TH
STRANGE
IMAGINATION
OF PIPPA CLAYTON

A heart-warming and original love story

By

Claire Gallagher

ISBN-13: 9798366641593

To Mark, with love.

CONTENTS

Chapter One

I smooth the *Berry Blush* gloss over my lips and make a popping sound as I rub them together. The livid red smears and I scowl at my reflection. Vanessa Vamp, the cartoon bombshell who is sitting on my shoulder, legs crossed seductively and unforgivably shiny crimson hair cascading deliciously over one shoulder, giggles at my ineptitude. I stick my tongue out at her and wipe away the greasy makeup, ready for attempt number two.

"You know, you wouldn't be able to balance in real life with proportions like that," I mutter at her spitefully, examining her ridiculously tiny waist and exaggerated bottom with a disapproving frown. She flicks her hair and pretends she hasn't heard me. "Not that men seem to care about that sort of thing – logic, I mean."

I stand back and examine myself in the full-length mirror which is next to the tiny bath tub. *Not bad,* I tell myself. *You'll do.* Vanessa winks at me. I'm wearing a classic Little Black Dress and strappy black heels. My dark brown hair is pulled into a chignon with little wisps loose around my face (not my own work – being useless with hair, I got my hairdresser to style it for me, tonight being a special occasion and all).

Smoky eyeshadow makes my eyes seem bluer than they really are, and my toenails and fingernails match my lips – again, not my work. Thank God for salons. *Beauty School Drop-Out* plays as I watch my reflection twirl.

Tonight is the office Christmas party. I'm employed by an advertising agency, MacKay Lexington of London, New York and, lately, Paris, if you please. But it's not as glamorous as it sounds – I'm a receptionist. Vanessa doesn't mind; she gets to lounge around all day, pouting and looking sexy for the clients. That's when she bothers to show up, which isn't always the case. When she *is* around, I mostly ignore her, the wanton hussy.

My phone dings with a message to inform me that my cab has arrived, so I grab my clutch bag and quickly go around switching off most of the lights in my little flat. I love my flat. It's my safe place. Even though it takes up most of my salary, I'm proud of the way I've made it my own – with colourful throws and scatter cushions, fairy lights and framed posters with motivational slogans.

Live, Love, Laugh

Keep Calm and Drink Coffee!

Believe You Can and You're Half-way There

There used to be others, but I took them down after …

Just, after.

The taxi driver beeps his horn and I curse him as I rush down the stairs and my right foot twists over on my heel as I reach the bottom. "I'm alright – I'm absolutely fine!" I tell Vanessa as I yank down my dress which has ridden up my thighs and pull open the door.

I clamber awkwardly into the waiting vehicle and give the address of the bar where the party is being held. Vanessa checks out the driver but he's around sixty and, disappointed, she pouts and settles down for a nap. I sigh and rest my head back as the car begins the twenty-minute journey. I could murder a G&T but I promised myself I would take it slowly this year after last year's debacle – they couldn't get me off the karaoke until I tripped over the mike stand and fell off the stage. It took three people to get me up off the floor.

This year I promise myself, *I will be classy and elegant. As cool as a cucumber. A graceful swan.* I close my eyes and remind myself why, this year in particular, I must be on my best behaviour – Tom Arnold. No, not the American comedian and actor. Tom Arnold is the new creative director at MacKay Lexington. I picture him in my mind's eye – all curly black hair, dimpled chin and designer glasses. Yummy.

Etta James starts singing *I Just Wanna Make Love to You* and Vanessa wakes up. She stretches, and I snort at her suddenly wide awake and lustful expression. The driver gives me an odd glance in the mirror, and I tut and mutter something incomprehensible about 'pedestrians' that even I can't understand.

I spend the rest of the journey staring out the side window, wilfully ignoring the shenanigans of Vanessa, who dances seductively on my shoulder to the music.

We finally arrive, and I thank the driver and pay him before climbing out of the cab and once again yanking my damned dress down. It's dark and cold and my breath fogs in the frigid air. I wrap my arms around myself and totter towards the bar where the smokers are already gathered outside getting their first hit of nicotine of the evening. The vapours form cartoon clouds of smoke that dissipate into the air.

"Hello! Hello!" I reply to the chorus of *Hello, Pips* as I scurry past them and into the warm interior of the venue. We have the whole place to ourselves and it looks like most people have already arrived, judging by the crowd. I rub the last of the bitter cold out of my arms and look around for Tim and Lucy before spying them in a booth.

It's a 'no partners' night so neither of them has brought their other half along, for which I'm grateful. It's no fun being the gooseberry. Not that they don't make an effort to include me when we all go out together – it's just naturally awkward being the odd-one-out all the time. Tables in restaurants always seem to have an even number of chairs, so there's always an empty seat, and an odd number of people makes buying rounds and splitting the bill trickier.

Lucy beams when she spots me weaving my way towards them, but Tim doesn't notice at first. When I arrive and he finally looks up from where he was glowering down at the table (where, I notice, their glasses are nearly empty already), he manages to lift the corner of his mouth in a cross between a smile and a grimace. I raise my eyebrows at Lucy and she shakes her spiky blonde head and hugs me.

"He's split up with Gloria," she murmurs in my ear, and I sigh. Hall and Oates start singing *Maneater* and I wave them away. It just looks like I'm flicking my hair off my shoulder, so nobody reacts, although my friends are used to some of my quirky little habits and probably wouldn't have batted an eyelid anyway.

"What happened?" I ask him, as I reach over to hug him too.

"It just wasn't working out," he answers, running his hand through his ginger hair. "I realised there wasn't that *spark*."

"*You've* dumped *her*?" I respond in surprise, and he gives a sharp nod.

"Wow," I say, and Dionne Warwick pops up and starts singing *Heartbreaker*. I ignore her. Lucy gives me a meaningful look, and I purse my lips in acknowledgement. Neither of us particularly liked Glamorous Gloria, and we had our suspicions about her fidelity, but Tim had seemed smitten, at least in the early days. "I think we all need a drink," I say authoritatively, my earlier promise to myself to take it steady already going out the window. I picture myself booting the word 'promise', which is written in bright red bubble writing, out of the front window of the venue, shattering the glass and scattering the smokers.

I make my way over to the bar, thinking that at least now I won't keep hearing Laura Branigan belting out *Gloria*, which happened every time I encountered Tim's – now ex – girlfriend.

Tom Arnold is already waiting at the bar when I arrive, and Vanessa purrs loudly when she spots him. I ignore the slut and stand next to him, waiting for him to notice me, bopping my head slightly to Andy Williams singing *Can't Take My Eyes Off You*. At last, he turns and smiles at me.

"Pip! You look lovely," he tells me with an appreciative

glance. I simper.

"So do you," I tell him, attempting to bat my eyelids like Vanessa would.

"Have you got something in your eye?" he frowns.

"Contact lens is playing up," I mutter.

"I didn't know you wore contacts," he says in surprise.

"*All the better to see you with, my dear,*" I respond in a deep voice, and he gives me a strange look.

I clear my throat. "It's a free bar tonight, isn't it?"

"Until ten," he confirms with a nod, and thankfully the bartender arrives and we place our orders. We wait awkwardly for the drinks and, when they finally arrive, I mumble a quick goodbye and carry the G&Ts back to the booth.

"Saw you talking to Tom," Lucy says slyly as I place the drinks down on the table.

"Yes," I say breezily. "And I was as cool as a cucumber."

"Yeah, right," she snorts, and we giggle. Tim sniggers.

"So, who's going to get off with who this year?" Lucy asks. "Place your bets."

"Evie and Mike," Tim says immediately.

"No way!" I tell him. "She wouldn't touch him with a barge pole!"

"I'm telling you, wait and see. There's a vibe between them."

"Is this your 'male intuition' at work?" I say with my tongue in my cheek. Tim is notorious for choosing the wrong kind of women.

"Call it what you want."

"I'm betting on Stan and Llewellyn," Lucy pipes up. "They've been flirting for years."

"You say them every year," I remind her.

"Well, it's *bound* to happen one of these years," she says defensively. "They just need a little nudge." She bites her lip before resolutely grabbing her drink and jumping up. Before we know it, she's marching over to where Stan and Llewellyn are studiously ignoring each other next to the dance floor, her piercings gleaming under the lights. She strikes up a conversation and soon gets them both talking. The sisters from *Fiddler on the Roof* start singing *Matchmaker* and I snort my drink out of my nose.

"Anything to win a bet," Tim smirks, ignoring my behaviour, and I click my tongue and hum my agreement.

"So, how did you end it with Gloria?" I ask curiously. I've never known him to be the one to end a relationship. He usually seems oblivious to their (cross out as appropriate) shallowness/vanity/wandering eye/selfishness/laziness/bitchiness, and it takes *them* calling it a day for him to stop plying them with gifts and realise that there's something missing.

"I just invited her round to mine for a drink and told her it wasn't working."

"How did she take it?"

He grimaces.

"Oh, like that."

He nods.

"How many smashed glasses?"

"None – but I had my own drink thrown in my face."

"Classic."

He shakes his head. "I'm vowing to stay single for at least six months."

"You say that after every relationship but within a week you're with the next girl." Objectively, Tim's a good-looking guy, and never has a problem getting a girlfriend.

"I mean it this time," he insists, and I raise my eyebrow, a trick I'm rather proud of.

"I do!"

"Okay!"

We watch the few brave souls on the dance floor for a few minutes, before Lucy re-joins us.

"I've done all I can," she announces. "The rest is up to them." We look over at Stan and Llewellyn. They're ignoring each other again. Lucy sighs. "Men!"

"You never said who *you're* betting on," Tim reminds me, and I pretend to think for a minute. Vanessa waits impatiently.

"Why, me and Tom, of course!" I finally declare triumphantly, and they roll their eyes.

"Well, it could happen," I say defensively.

"Would you though?" Tim asks me gently. "Even if you could get over your laughable awkwardness around him? Are you ... ready?"

"Course I am," I answer breezily, and toss back the last of my G&T before heading back to the bar for another round. Vanessa growls at me, and I flick her away. For once, she vanishes.

The rest of the evening goes as you've probably predicted. The CEO gives a speech, followed by a better one from Tom Arnold; I drink far too many G&Ts and end up once again on the karaoke, murdering Gloria Gaynor's *I Will Survive*, but at least I get myself off the stage in one piece after just the one performance; Tim and Lucy finally tip me into a cab at two a.m. and I go home and fall into a dead sleep without removing my clothes or makeup, while Bill Medley and Jennifer Warnes croon *I've Had The Time of My Life* quietly in the background.

Chapter Two

The next day is Sunday, and I have a hangover. I spend the day drinking copious amounts of water and watching re-runs of *Friends* (*I'll Be There For Yo-ou!*) while snuggled under my duvet on the sofa. My cat, Mr. Fluffles, sits on top of my hip, purring, and Vanessa is nowhere to be seen.

Chapter Three

M onday sees me bright and fresh at my desk. It's a week until Christmas. I'm wearing a Santa hat and I've decorated my domain with a little tree and a cheery garland as usual. People greet me more warmly now that the festive season is here and I marvel at the difference the occasion makes to the normally stern and serious clients as they arrive in the open-plan office.

I spend the morning answering the phone, transferring calls and fetching coffees for important clients, while Dolly Parton chirpily warbles *9 To 5*, then meet up with Tim and Lucy for lunch. They're both account managers and they spend most of the time trying to out-do each other in a contest of whose clients are the biggest pain in the arse.

The afternoon is quieter and I spend the lulls between traffic sketching out story boards for ad campaigns that we're currently trying to win. It's not in my job description, and no one sees them except for me, but I have an art degree and it passes the time. At the moment, I'm working on a series of frames for Lexus showing the *Xi* model cruising through the City, its reflection repeated countless times in the mirrored windows of the buildings. I use monochrome lines to illustrate the fast-paced action of the car, and stick my tongue out the side of my mouth as I work. Vanessa purrs at the sleek machine, and I nod to the rhythm of *Fast Car* by Tracy Chapman as sequences of thought bubbles with my sketches inside appear above my head.

The sound of someone clearing their throat makes me jerk my head up and my jaw drops as the most beautiful man I've ever seen quirks an eyebrow at me. How long he's been standing there I have no idea and I blush as I realise that I'm staring at him without speaking. Little pink and red hearts appear and pop around his head. I lurch to my feet.

"Good afternoon," I breathe. "Welcome to MacKay Lexington. How may I help you?"

"Max Wild," he smirks. "To see Tom Arnold." He has an Australian accent and – I swear – his hair is *gold*.

"M-Max Wild, of course! Please, take a seat and I'll let Mr. Arnold know that you're here."

He moves towards the seating area, and I buzz through to Tom.

"May I offer you tea, coffee, water?" I gush at Mr. Wild as Donna Summer starts belting out *Hot Stuff* and Vanessa practically drools over my shoulder.

"I'll take a coffee – please," he twinkles those baby blues at me, and, for a second, I forget my own name.

"Coffee?" My voice goes up on the second syllable for some reason, and I cover for it quickly. "Of course, you can have coffee!"

"White – no sugar," he tells me as I remain standing in

front of him like an idiot.

"White – no sugar," I repeat. "Right." And after another pause, I turn-tail and scamper away to the kitchen.

I return with the drink in a chic cup and saucer just as Tom appears and shakes Max's hand. Seeing them together is like seeing two Greek gods on Mount Olympus and I almost swoon. Vanessa mews like a cat and flicks her hair enticingly over her shoulder. *Attention seeker*, I think at her, but she pouts and ignores me. Barbara Streisand bursts into *Woman in Love* at full volume and I'm tempted to join in, but bite my lip and manage to resist.

Max Wild is head honcho at Wild Spirit Inc. and MacKay Lexington has been trying to land him as a client since forever, without success. There have been rumours that he's shopping around for a new ad agency, and I guess his appearance today signals that it's not just the usual industry gossip. I wonder what product he wants to advertise and itch with anticipation at the thought of storyboarding my ideas for it.

I arrive beside them with the coffee, and Max takes it from me with a smile. He looks at my name badge. "Thank you, Pippa Clayton," he smiles, and I blush. He takes a sip and smacks his lips together in appreciation. "Talented at making coffee *and* designing ads. I'm impressed already, Arnold, and I haven't even got past the receptionist," he says to Tom, who frowns in confusion. I smile frozenly, then realise I'm blocking their way and scurry back behind my desk. They head off to Tom's office and Max looks back at me lingeringly before the door closes. I take a deep breath and Vanessa pouts at the loss of male attention.

They're in Tom's office for over an hour. It's glass-fronted, so I can see them the whole time. They spend much of the time in earnest conversation, though there's the occasional laugh, and I can see that Max likes Tom. He has the right mix of charm and sincerity, and he's really *good* at his job. I'm proud of him for representing our agency so well.

At one point, about half an hour in, Tom suddenly turns to look at me with a surprised expression, and I quickly pick up the phone and pretend to talk while Vanessa blows him a kiss. When I look back, he's turned away, and I breathe a sigh of relief.

At ten past four, they're done. Tom escorts Max to the lift and they shake hands. The latter makes a point of raising his hand to say goodbye to me, and I hear panting in my ear as he winks. I nod jerkily and breathe a weak 'Cheerio!' as the doors slide shut on him.

Tom slowly makes his way back towards his office, a thoughtful frown on his face. I pull my storyboard sketches out from under the papers I'd shoved them beneath when I became aware of Max's presence, and spend the rest of the hour daydreaming and doodling, humming along while the Carpenters sing *Close To You*.

At five, I gather my things and head for the bus stop. The journey home takes forty minutes, and I sigh when a man sits next to me within minutes and spreads his knees wide apart. Vanessa huffs and I imagine myself doing something outrageous to scare him into moving to a different seat, something like channelling Kate Bush and bursting into *Wuthering Heights* at the top of my voice, freaky arm movements and all, but I haven't got the guts.

When I get off at my stop, I decide to pick up a Chinese take-out. I order a twenty-seven and fifty-three (spring rolls and chicken chow mein) then sit down to browse through a magazine while waiting. It's all celebrity news and Royal Family dramas and I soon get lost in the juicy gossip until I hear a familiar voice ordering the *exact* same numbers as me. Vanessa's ears perk up too and we simultaneously swivel our heads like satellite dishes towards the smooth-as-chocolate voice. Tom Arnold stands at the counter, his back towards me, but I'd recognise that pert butt anywhere.

He finally turns and takes a seat without looking at me. I stare at him, waiting for him to see me, and Vanessa does the same. The minutes drag on and I begin to get strange looks from the other customers. I hear the *Countdown* tune ticking away and I remind myself to blink. At last, he glances over at me and I give my head a little shake and quickly school my expression into one of astonished surprise. "Tom!" I cry as if in unexpected delight. "Fancy seeing you here!"

"Pippa! I didn't know you lived around here!" he replies in equal surprise.

"*All the better to stalk you, my dear,*" I say in a deep voice before clamping my lips firmly closed. I feel my cheeks redden.

Tom chuckles awkwardly then gestures at the board displaying the menu. "What're you having?"

"Twenty-seven and fifty-three," I tell him proudly, and wait for his reaction.

"Me too!" he answers.

I open my mouth in shock. "No way!"

"Great minds think alike."

"They do," I nod wisely. We sit in silence for a moment.

"Do you come here often?" I ask at last.

"About once a month, as a treat."

"Me too," I lie – it's more like once a week if I'm honest. "Good spring rolls," I add, and Vanessa sighs.

"Hmm," he agrees. Another silence. Then, "Actually, I was going to leave a note on your desk for you tomorrow morning asking you to come and see me – might as well tell you now since we're here."

"Oh?" I question, and I feel the little frown line appear between my eyebrows.

"Nothing to worry about," he reassures me, but I instantly envision a box packed with my belongings from my desk and two security guards kicking me out of the building. I stumble through the revolving doors and land flat on my face, the contents of the box scattering, my skirt flying up to reveal my tired old granny knickers. I blink, and paste a wide smile on my face as if I'm completely reassured, but it must be a bit *too* wide because he frowns and gives me a strange look. At that moment, my order is declared ready. He tells me that he'll get Lisa to cover reception at ten o'clock the following morning and we say our goodbyes. I scuttle out of the shop to the tune of *It's The End Of The World As We Know It* by R.E.M. Vanessa looks back from my shoulder, waving prettily. "Slut," I tell her grumpily, and she smirks.

I give in and buy a bottle of wine from the off-licence, and spend the five-minute walk to my flat updating my CV. The words appear above my head, like lines of type, as I walk down the street with my bags.

Name: Pippa Clayton

Age: 31

Email address: nobodyputsbabyinthecorner@hotmail.com

Personal Qualities: I have low expectations of myself and a tendency to go for 'safe' jobs that won't challenge me, in case I screw up and people realise that I'm an imposter impersonating someone who *actually* knows what they're doing.

Education and Qualifications: Art degree (2:1 because I was too busy partying to give 100%).

Work Experience: Bar work and admin jobs – lots! Too boring to go into details.

Hobbies and Interests: Delicately eating all the chocolate off a Kit Kat before consuming the wafer. Talking to an imaginary character who sits on my shoulder. Hearing a soundtrack to my life. Doesn't everyone?

Depressed, I reach my front door, insert the key into the lock and head straight to the tiny kitchen for the corkscrew. I don't bother with a glass, just pour from the bottle straight into my wide-open mouth. It dribbles down my chin but I keep gulping loudly at the delicious nectar. I only stop when I need to breathe. Gasping, I wipe my mouth with the back of my hand and delicately stifle a burp.

I lay the contents of the bag out on the counter and peel off the lids. The sumptuous aroma of greasy food permeates the air and I grab a fork and start eating straight from the trays. Vanessa has gone, and I am all alone. But no, Celine Dion does *not* start bleating *All By Myself* – that's someone else's story. Instead, Radiohead sing *No Surprises,* and I stare at the kitchen wall.

The spell is broken when Mr. Fluffles starts weaving between my legs and rubbing himself against me, reminding me to feed him. "Okay, okay, buddy," I tell him and then I go flying on some spilled wine as I move to get his food from the cupboard. I land on my back, hard, and lie there staring up at the ceiling, dazed. Mr. Fluffles nudges my face, and I start stroking his silky black fur. He licks me, his tongue rough, and I realise that I have become 'the cat lady' that I swore I would never be. I sigh and pull myself up, rubbing the back of my head as I make my way over to the freezer to grab a packet of peas. I use a bandage to tie them onto my head, knotting it under my chin, and that's when the doorbell goes.

I pull the door open and Lucy walks in. She doesn't even blink at my strange appearance as she stalks past me into the kitchen. She spots the wine and grabs it, tipping it up and necking it down in almost exactly the same way I did. I grab some kitchen towel and clear up the spillage before finally forking food into Mr. Fluffles' bowl. He meows loudly while I'm working. Lucy drinks the whole time, and eventually I prise the bottle away from her and ask her what's wrong.

"Miranda," is the only answer I get before she's snatching the bottle back off me and lifting it towards her lips. I wrestle it away from her and put it out of reach. She scowls at me.

"What about Miranda?" I ask. "You've barely had time to

get home from work – surely you can't have had an argument already?"

"She told me she was going to be working late."

"So?"

"So, if she's working late, how come I saw her in a restaurant with Phoebe?"

"Oh." I take the bottle back down from on top of the fridge-freezer and take a large swig then pass it back to her. "Tell me everything."

She does. It turns out that Lucy had decided on the spur of the moment to visit her mother after work. When she'd left the tube station, she'd had to walk past the restaurant in question, and had seen them through the window, looking *very* cosy. I picture the scene, and Atlantic Starr start singing *Secret Lovers*.

Phoebe is Miranda's ex, and they're still good friends. It's the only thing that the two of them argue about.

"She could have a perfectly good explanation," I tell her gently, as she starts in on my leftover chow mein.

"For *lying* to me?" she growls around a mouthful of Chinese food, and I grimace. It does seem dodgy.

I spend the rest of the evening trying to persuade her to go home and talk it through, but Lucy is stubborn, and she ends up falling asleep half-drunk on my sofa while we're watching re-runs of *Frasier*. I put a blanket over her and turn in for the night, almost – but not quite – forgetting about my meeting with Tom tomorrow.

Chapter Four

A t seven a.m. I nudge Lucy awake and hand her a cup of
tea before heading for the shower. While I'm washing my
hair, Frank Sinatra sings *My Way* and I swear at him rudely. I
try to force a change to *Don't Worry, Be Happy* by Bobby
McFerrin and a battle of wills ensues as the soundtrack flips
between the two. I join in with my preference at the top of my
lungs until Lucy bangs on the door.

"Christ! Are you strangling Mr. Fluffles in there?"

The music screeches to a stop, and I shout "Sorry!"
sheepishly.

We switch over, and I head to my room to get dressed and
dry my hair. Vanessa is lounging on my bed, long legs curled to
the side of her, head resting on her hand, examining her nails.

"No nonsense from you today, madam," I tell her as I pull
my underwear out of the drawer and start putting it on. "I
need you to be on your *best* behaviour." She pulls her most
innocent expression, and I purse my lips, not buying the act
for a second. "He may be one of the sexiest men we've ever
met, but I need to be focussed and professional – after all, my
job might be on the line." I stand there with my hands on my

hips, my most serious expression on my face, and it's then that I notice my reflection in the mirror. I have my polka dot knickers on back-to-front. Vanessa giggles, and I huff, hurrying to switch them around.

I finish getting ready and help Lucy to pick something out of my wardrobe to wear. She's edgier than me, but she manages to find a combination of clothes that works for her. We grab some toast then I give her a spare toothbrush and, dangerously, full access to my makeup bag. By eight o'clock, we're heading out the door to the bus stop.

"What are you going to do about Miranda?" I finally muster the courage to ask gently.

She bites her lip and shakes her head. I sigh and decide to drop the subject rather than re-hashing my arguments of the night before.

I change the subject. "Tom Arnold wants to see me at ten."

She looks at me in surprise. "What for?"

"I don't know." I feel the little frown line appear between my eyebrows. Lucy notices.

"I'm sure it's nothing to worry about."

"That's what I'm trying to tell myself."

She pats me on the shoulder as the bus rounds the corner. "Let me know how it goes." I nod.

We spend the forty-minute journey debating the best way to eat a Kit Kat, which morphs into an argument over the best way to eat a Bounty. Lucy is all for snapping them in half then biting them, so the whole experience is over within seconds. I scorn her lack of finesse, and we nearly come to blows before we stop and burst into hysterical laughter. A man across the aisle gives us a strange look, and we laugh even harder.

We get off the bus and walk the short distance to the office. At my desk we hug goodbye, and she murmurs another admonishment not to worry. I nod, but I'm chewing my lip to pieces.

Fortunately, at nine on the dot, the phone starts ringing and I have no time to fret as I spend the next half an hour fielding non-stop calls and clients.

There's a lull at 9:30, and I sit biting my nails and staring at the clock as the hands tick steadily closer to ten.

Tim appears at a quarter to, and I paste on an overly bright smile so he won't suspect anything's wrong. Luckily, he's too preoccupied with his news to notice.

"I've met the one," he announces.

"Which one?"

"*The* one."

"Oh, *that* one."

He nods like an eager puppy and a zealous light shines in his eyes.

I sigh. "You say this every time you meet someone new."

"It's different this time."

"You say that too."

"I mean it."

"Okay. Spill the beans then. Tell me all about her."

"Her name's Roxanne." Cue The Police (why does he always go for women whose names are song titles?). "She's a –" *prostitute* "– waitress. She's twenty-six. She likes –" *walking the streets for money* "– ice skating and yoga and her favourite colour is –" *red* "– yellow." He beams and pauses for breath.

"She sounds ... great!" I half-grimace, half smile. He lost me at yoga (shudder). I attended a yoga session once; I fell asleep during the meditation part and my own snoring woke me up. The instructor was not amused. Neither was I – I couldn't walk comfortably for a whole week afterwards.

"She *is* great," Tim agrees enthusiastically.

"Where did you meet her?"

"At the ice rink last night. I went with my sister and nephew. We *literally* bumped into each other – isn't that funny?

"Hilarious."

"Great story for the grandkids," he agrees, and this time I really do grimace.

"I took her for a drink after and we're seeing each other again tomorrow night," Tim continues obliviously.

"That's nice, but ... maybe take it more *slowly* this time, yeah?" I say gently.

He frowns seriously. "Right, right ... play hard to get?"

"Well – hard*er* at least."

"Hmm, you might be on to something. Don't want to come on too strongly. Come across as too desperate."

"Exactly," I beam. And if she's anything as shallow as his

previous girlfriends, maybe he won't be taken for a mug this time, I think.

He ponders for a moment. "I should return the necklace I bought her."

"Probably a good idea," I agree.

"Get her a bracelet instead."

"Or ..."

"Or ... earrings?"

"Or *nothing* ... yet. Don't want to come on too strongly – remember?"

"Yes, yes. You're right. I'm playing 'hard to get Tim'," he nods earnestly.

"That's right," I nod along and widen my eyes for emphasis.

When Lisa shows up, we're still doing our nodding dog act at each other. She clears her throat, and I jump. Lisa sighs impatiently. She's Tom's PA, and I know that she sees working reception as beneath her, and so does Vanessa, who sticks her tongue out at her. I paste on a professional smile and say goodbye to Tim.

"Alright, Lisa?" I say, as I take my leave.

"I think I can handle it," she smirks. I give her my best fake smile and spitefully hope that she gets inundated with awkward calls and difficult clients.

I nip to the loo before heading to Tom's office although I don't really need it. I spend a few minutes fiddling with my hair in the mirror and re-touching my lip gloss, trying to delay the inevitable. When I can't think of anything else to do, I take a deep breath, and head for the door.

The walk to Tom's office seems to happen in slow motion, but all too soon I'm raising my hand to knock, and he looks up from his computer and waves for me to enter. I take another breath and push open the door.

Tom looks even more delicious than usual, if that's possible, and Hot Chocolate burst into *You Sexy Thing* as Vanessa and I stand gaping at him from the doorway. He cocks his head and a wrinkle appears between his eyebrows, deepening the longer I remain unmoving. I suddenly realise what I must look like, and give myself a little shake before moving further into the room, closing the door behind me. Vanessa purrs at him as I take a seat across from him.

"Pippa, thanks for coming," he says as I sit squirming. I cross my right leg over my left, then my left over my right, then pull the sleeves of my blouse down before pushing them back up. He watches me in confusion, and I realise that I haven't responded to him.

"Oh! No problem," I finally answer. I swipe at Vanessa to stop her panting in my ear.

"Did you enjoy your twenty-seven and fifty-three?"

"I *did* – did you?"

"Yes," he grimaces, "but I had to work harder in the gym this morning to make up for it." I picture him, all sweaty and gleaming from his workout, and practically swoon. Vanessa actually does.

"Do you work out? You look like you do," he continues.

"A bit," I lie, and resolve to go for a jog straight after work.

"I can tell."

"Thanks," I blush.

He clears his throat and places his hands on his desk. "Anyway, back to the matter at hand. There's something of great importance I need to discuss with you." And I hear my heart beating so loudly, I imagine it thudding out of my chest like in a cartoon love scene. Vanessa sits up straight on my shoulder, all ears.

"I don't quite know how to say this," he begins, "but I've got a rather unusual request." He frowns and looks at me doubtfully.

My eyebrows shoot up. "A request?"

"Mmm. It relates to Max Wild's visit yesterday."

"Max Wild's visit yesterday?" I repeat like an idiot, but I'm totally confused. After all, I'd half-expected to be made redundant, so this has come straight out of left field for me.

"Yes, he wants you to be part of the creative team that pitches for his latest ad – it's for his new flavoured vodka."

My jaw drops. "Me?" I finally manage to squeak.

He chuckles. "I can promise you that I was as surprised as you when he made the request."

"Why me?" I croak. I'm actually shaking.

"It seems that he spotted a talent that you've been keeping secret from us," he admonishes gently, and I feel my face redden yet again.

"Well, of course, I couldn't possible do it," I tell him as firmly as I can.

"He won't allow us to pitch if you're not on the team. He said it's non-negotiable. You made quite the impression, it seems." Is that a little jealousy I detect?

I open my mouth to answer, but I can't think of one, so I just shake my head and clamp it closed.

"I've looked at your file," he tells me softly. "You have an art degree, so you have some of the skills needed already. The team will help you with the rest."

"I can't," I say shakily, but I can feel myself wavering as I look into his chocolatey eyes. Queen start singing *Under Pressure*, and I gulp.

"Please? You'll get renumerated and it would mean *a lot* to win the business of Wild Spirit Inc."

And I can't refuse again. I nod stiffly, and for a second it's worth the smile that he beams at me.

"Excellent! We have a few months before the pitch so we'll start working on it after Christmas. Max wants to be involved as much as possible so you'll probably have a few meetings with him, which is great because he'll steer you in the direction he wants." He claps his hands and rubs them together, as if he can't wait to get started. I smile weakly, and the meeting is over. I stand on shaky legs and make my way to the door while Vanessa looks back, fluttering her eyelids at him.

As I make my way back to my desk, I wonder how I'm going to get through this without being discovered as the fraud I am. There's a big difference between doing a few doodles and creating a big ad campaign, and Max and Tom should know that. A little bit of sick comes up into my mouth.

Chapter Five

The rest of the week passes swiftly. Lucy remains my house guest and refuses to speak to Miranda, who calls constantly, begging to know what's going on. I help Lucy pick up some of her things one evening when Miranda is at an evening class and we soon settle into a routine.

Tim goes on his date with *Roxanne-you-don't-have-to-put-on-the-red-light!* and it's an unmitigated disaster. Apparently, he played it a little *too* hard to get – he deliberately turned up late, showed zero interest in getting to know her any better and instead spent the whole time talking about himself; and he left her to pay the bill before scooting off to the tube station and leaving her in the rain outside the restaurant. He tells me this proudly during Thursday's lunch break and I bang my head on the table.

"What?" he asks in innocent bemusement.

"Playing hard to get doesn't mean being a dick," I tell him, rubbing my forehead. Vanessa tuts.

"But you said not to come on too strongly."

"You can still be a gentleman without coming on too strongly. It's about getting the right balance."

"Oh." He thinks for a minute then slaps his head in horrified realisation. "Oh God! I've totally ruined my chances, haven't I?"

I grimace in acknowledgement, and he puts his head in his hands. "Perhaps the situation can still be recovered?" I suggest hopefully.

"I ate her dessert."

"Then it's *definitely* over."

We sigh.

"Back to the drawing board then, I guess," he says despondently. I wonder what song his next date will share a name with and place a secret bet on Tom Jones's *Delilah*.

I report the conversation back to Lucy on the bus ride home – she was too busy to join us for lunch – and she goes for *Cecilia*. Her phone rings when we're five minutes from home, but she ignores it when she sees Miranda's name on the screen.

"You're going to have to speak to her some time," I tell her gently, and she bites her lip and sighs.

Friday is the last day of work before the Christmas holiday and the office closes at one. At twelve-thirty, I help to give out glasses of champagne and we open our Secret Santa presents. I have been gifted with a set of Christmas tree earrings and a pair of socks which have 'Ho ho ho!' written on them. I suspect they're from Stan, who I see attempting to surreptitiously watch my reaction but failing dismally. I paste on a delighted smile and enthusiastically swap out my diamond earrings for the Christmas trees. I hope they won't turn my ear lobes green but I have my doubts.

During the week, I've been advertising 'Kisses for a Pound' to raise money for a donkey sanctuary and I'm pleased to say that I've raised nearly two hundred pounds. I have mistletoe hung over my desk and I'm behind it collecting my belongings when Tom approaches at ten past one. Most of the staff had made a hasty exit at one on the dot but I'd spent time loading the dishwasher so I'm still here. I look at him in surprise and his cheeks redden. He gestures to my sign. "Are you still collecting for the sanctuary?"

I nod, and he places a twenty-pound note in the basket and looks at me expectantly. I lean across the desk and kiss him softly on the corner of the mouth. He smells delicious – like some kind of tropical aftershave mixed with heady undertones of masculinity. Vanessa swoons, and I feel my legs tremble. I lean back, and he's looking at me strangely. Our gaze holds for a second too long, and that's when Llewellyn comes bustling over.

"Don't forget me!" he trills, and throws a coin into the basket. Tom clears his throat and steps back as I give Llewellyn his kiss. He beams, then engages Tom in a conversation about one of his accounts. I finish gathering my things then head over to the lift, wishing them a 'Merry Christmas!' as I pass. "You too – bye, love," says Llewellyn, and Tom murmurs, "Have a good one." The bell dings and I step in and turn around. Llewellyn is prattling on, but Tom is watching me. I smile tentatively at him and he gives a small smile back, then the doors close.

I use the afternoon to complete last minute shopping, then head home to pack my bag. I'm spending Christmas with my parents – I have a 10:15 train ticket for tomorrow, which is Christmas Eve – and Lucy is going to her brother's house. We spend the evening watching *Love Actually*, eating chocolates and drinking red wine before wishing each other a good night. She still hasn't spoken to Miranda.

The next morning, I exchange gifts with Lucy and hug her goodbye. She's putting on a brave face but I can tell that she's finding the festive period hard without Miranda. They've been together for three years and have spent every one of those Christmases together. "Call her, you stubborn bugger," I urge gently before I leave, but she shakes her head.

I arrive at the station at ten o'clock and board the waiting train. My reserved seat is taken and I picture myself lifting the culprit up bodily and throwing them out of it. They skid down the aisle and only stop when they bump into the automatic doors. Cartoon birds flit around their head and I brush my hands together repeatedly in a job well done as the rest of the passengers burst into applause. But, of course, I don't do that. Instead, I tut loudly and take a different seat, unable to relax because I expect at any moment that the seat's real owner will turn up and claim it aggressively.

The journey takes just over an hour. Vanessa is nowhere to be seen, so I spend it amusing myself by imagining that I'm on the *Hogwarts Express*, eating chocolate frogs and dodging Dementors. Steam billows past the windows and magical music echoes around the carriage. I find myself humming along and get more than one strange look but I don't care. It's Christmas, and there are things I don't want to think about, and if this is the way to keep my mind off unwelcome subjects, so be it. The alternative is far worse.

My dad is waiting for me at the station. "Hello, darling," he beams distractedly when he sees me, and we hug before heading to the car. He puts my bag in the boot of his old Jag and we head out into the countryside. My dad is a history lecturer at a university and his head is always in a different time – any but the modern day. He starts telling me about a research paper he's working on exploring medieval weaponry and its importance to cultural evolution. I nod along, not understanding half of the jargon he's using, and when he finally pauses for breath, I manage to ask how my mother is.

"She's fine," he tells me. "Hooked on her latest hobby, as usual."

"Which one is it this time?" I ask him to remind me; it changes so frequently, I can't keep up.

"Origami."

"Oh, yes."

"She's found an online community and they share their designs. She's always uploading photos. The house is full of the stuff."

"At least it keeps her busy." My mum is old-fashioned and stopped working as a typist when she married my dad thirty years ago. She belongs to all sorts of clubs and social groups, and volunteers as an entertainment co-ordinator at a local old people's home. She gets them playing Bingo and holds sing-a-longs. She's a force of nature.

"Oh, she's busy alright. Best thing to be. Stops people

thinking too much." He glances over at me as he steers. "Are *you* keeping yourself busy, love?" he asks in a softer voice, and I nod stiffly. He knows better than to ask any further and reaches over to put the radio on. Aptly, Chris Rea is singing *Driving Home for Christmas,* and we smile at each other and the tension is broken.

Mum comes running out the door of their house as the car pulls up. "There you are, darling!" she gushes and gives me air kisses on each cheek. She links arms with me and guides me inside as Dad collects my bag from the boot. "I've been absolutely *dying* to show you my creations," she continues proudly, and I tell her that I can't *wait* to see them.

We enter the house and they're literally everywhere – on the windowsills, on the mantle, on the coffee table, even hung up on string on the walls. I turn to Dad, who has just come in behind us, and widen my eyes. He chuckles.

"Wow!" I say, and Mum beams. I examine them more closely and see that she has a preference for making animals – there are birds, tortoises, butterflies, squirrels, cats and elephants to name a few. But here and there are a few oddities – I spot Yoda and Darth Vader arranged in a group with a monkey and a dragon. The whole thing is obviously bizarre, but they're actually quite sweet and she's clearly spent a lot of time perfecting the craft. I can see it makes her happy, so I tell her I'm impressed. She positively glows. Dad winks at me.

As usual, Mum has prepared a buffet for my return as if she's planning on feeding the five thousand. I stuff myself on prawn and mayo sandwiches, sausage rolls and pork pie, then head to unpack my bag. My room is exactly the same as it was when I left home at eighteen to attend university. There are still fan-girl posters on the wall and a yin and yang quilt cover on the bed. I cringe as I spot the reminders of the gawky teenager I once was, before I remember that the gawky teenager just turned into an equally gawky adult.

After I've unpacked, I take a nap, then spend some time in the shed with my dad while he works on his wine-making. Demijohns already bubble away, and he sucks on a tube to transfer the liquid from one container to another. It's relaxing to sit on a rickety old table and watch him pottering away, his pipe in his mouth, while UB40 sing *Red, Red Wine* in my head. He gives me some samples to try, and I grade them out of ten for their sweetness and body. Mum joins us after a while, and by the end of the session the two of us are more than a little tipsy. She decides to teach me how to make an origami swan, and we go into the house and sit in the kitchen folding paper and giggling before finishing off the buffet for tea.

The evening is spent watching *A Christmas Carol*, which is a Christmas Eve tradition in my family. I love the way that Scrooge is redeemed; it gives me hope that it's never too late for good things to happen.

At 10:30, we kiss each other goodnight and I fall asleep with Vanessa curled against me. She has been especially calm and content today, and I think she's trying to be considerate given how hard I find the festive period. We snuggle under the covers and although the room is slightly too warm, I fall into a deep and dreamless sleep.

Mum wakes me at eight the next morning, excited to see me open my presents, like I'm still seven years old. I humour her and pad downstairs in my pyjamas, greeting my dad, who's likewise been prised out of bed, with a "Merry Christmas, Dad" and a peck on the cheek. Festive music is already playing on the stereo and our presents are arranged in piles – one for each of us. I laugh at the family tradition and add my own gifts to my mum and dad's piles as Mum brings bacon sandwiches through from the kitchen.

We eat and open our presents at the same time. Among other gifts, I receive my favourite perfume and a book called *The Art of Origami*. Mum is pleased with her handbag and Dad loves the pocket watch I spent ages hunting down for him. We have a glass of champagne and then head to get dressed.

We work as a team to prepare Christmas dinner for seven people. My auntie Joy and uncle Vernon are coming over, together with a neighbour called Margaret who has no family, and a lecturer friend of Dad's called Arthur. I have my suspicions that Mum is up to a bit of matchmaking between them and I cringe in readiness for her less-than-subtle hints.

They're expected at one, and the doorbell rings at five to. I open the door to Joy and Vernon, and I've forgotten how tactless they are until my aunt cries, "There you are, you poor thing!" She hugs me, and I'm surrounded by the scent of lavender – it's so strong that I start coughing and my eyes water. She pats me on the back and tells me I'm all skin and bones. She turns to my uncle. "Isn't she thin, Vernon?" He grunts and tells me I need more meat on my bones.

Joy tuts. "It's no use starving yourself – that won't bring him back." I freeze, my face a mask, and Mum comes bustling over to lead her sister-in-law away. She starts chattering on about her origami and my aunt follows her around, examining the exhibits, her mouth pursed like she's eaten a lemon. Vernon stares at the paper menagerie in bemusement and the doorbell rings again.

Margaret is waiting on the doorstep, and as usual she has the expression of a dog that's been kicked too many times. I wish her a merry Christmas and take her coat before leaving her with Dad, while I hurry to pour drinks for everyone.

The doorbell goes for the last time as Arthur arrives. He's younger than I expected – in his forties, whereas Margaret is in her early sixties. His eyes light up when he sees me, and my heart sinks as I realise that Mum's matchmaking is not intended for her neighbour.

Chapter Six

The guests mingle and I feel Arthur's eyes on me as I make small talk with Margaret. Margaret is a widow and her sole topics of conversation are her latest health problem (piles this time), her dogs (Patsy and Susie, the fattest and laziest pooches I've ever seen) and her late husband, Alan (whom she has nothing good to say about but insists on telling me about him anyway). He had a heart attack while he was on the toilet and his mistress turned up at the funeral. She reminds me of this every time we meet.

"You're lucky if you can find a good one," she tells me morosely.

"Hmm," I murmur. Then, "Can I get you another glass of port, Margaret?" She nods, and with relief I hustle to the kitchen.

Dad is in there pouring himself another whiskey, and he gives me a sympathetic look. "Saw you speaking to Margaret. I know it's hard, but be patient. She's a very lonely woman."

I sigh. "I know." And he gives me a meaningful glance which I ignore.

He changes the subject. "Have you had a chance to speak

to Arthur yet? He's an interesting fellow. Has a PhD in Plantagenet family life."

I pull a face. "No, I haven't. And I know what you and Mum are up to and you can stop it right now."

He gives me his most innocent look. "I don't know what you're talking about. His family are all in Scotland and he was going to spend Christmas on his own. It was the charitable thing to do."

"Hmm," I say doubtfully with my eyebrow raised. He chuckles and I cluck my tongue.

We head back to the lounge and I hand Margaret her drink. She's talking to Joy now, and I can tell from my aunt's face that she's in the middle of telling her about her piles problem. Mum comes over at that moment and drags me over to meet Arthur properly. I smile at him politely and take a sip of my drink. He's not an unpleasant looking man, but rather non-descript, and he does nothing for me. Vanessa took one look at him and went back to sleep. Mum starts gushing about my job in London, making it sound much more glamorous than it is, and I feel my cheeks redden. Within minutes, she pretends to hear my dad calling her and gives me a sly look as she bustles off. Arthur and I stare at each other uncomfortably for a moment.

"So, you have a PhD in –?" I begin.

"It must be pretty exciting living in –" he starts.

We both stop and laugh.

"You go first," he tells me.

"My dad says you have a PhD in the Plantagenets?" I school my expression into one of polite interest.

He waves this away. "It's okay," he says drily. "I won't make you suffer by telling you all about that." He smiles, and I immediately warm to him. He asks me a few questions about my own interests, and we discover that we've been to some of the same concerts. He stays away from awkward topics, and I begin to relax, the shallowness of the conversation suiting me. I see Mum give Dad a knowing look and I roll my eyes at him when Arthur's not looking. He winks at me.

Soon it's time to sit down for our Christmas dinner, and I help to place the steaming dishes on the table that I set earlier. Everyone oohs their appreciation as the turkey is put down in the centre, and Dad starts carving. Wizard plays on the stereo.

Mum has craftily manipulated a place for Arthur next to me, and uncle Vernon sits on my other side. Auntie Joy warns him loudly against eating the sprouts – he has a flatulence problem – and I bite my tongue to stop myself from laughing. Vanessa has woken up and she wrinkles her nose in disgust. Vernon turns red.

Dad takes pity on him and starts a conversation on Christmas traditions in medieval times – no turkey or Christmas trees apparently – and we all tuck in. Wizard morphs into Slade and Mum gives me an exaggeratedly impressed look as Arthur adds his knowledge of Plantagenet traditions to the discussion. I widen my eyes and nod at her, and this satisfies her.

I feel safe with this topic of conversation, but I can tell that Joy is getting impatient. I take a swig of my drink and brace myself.

"No young man on the scene at the moment, Pippa?" she cuts across the conversation abruptly to ask. I feel Arthur's eyes on me and my mum gives my dad a nervous glance. She opens her mouth to speak but Joy continues. "You're not getting any younger, you know. Don't you want babies?"

There's a long pause. Mum looks horrified. Then Arthur breaks into a coughing fit and knocks over his wine glass. "I'm so sorry!" he splutters as everyone leaps up and I rush to fetch a cloth. I busy myself wiping up every drop and re-filling his glass, murmuring "Thank you" when the conversation moves on to a new topic, helped along by Mum and Dad. I lose my appetite after that and take to finishing off the bottle of wine that's in front of me.

We move on to dessert – Christmas pudding and custard – but I decide to drink mine. Margaret starts talking about the Christmas when Alan had diarrhoea, and Arthur also reaches for the bottle. Everyone except Margaret soon decides they've had enough of their pudding and one spoon after another clatters into the bowls in quick succession. Mum tries repeatedly to steer the conversation in another direction but Margaret is oblivious and continues her monologue.

I'm feeling more than a little drunk by this time, and Johnny Cash has started singing *Ring of Fire* in my head. I catch Dad's eye and giggle. Vernon looks at me strangely but I don't care. I hear Arthur snort and cover it with a cough and this makes me giggle even harder. Soon I am laughing uncontrollably and I can't stop. Tears leak out of my eyes and I can barely breathe. I feel my face turn bright red. The laughing turns to cackling, and I still can't stop. I'm aware that everyone has frozen and are staring at me, but their shocked faces just add fuel to the fire. Eventually, my dad gets up and comes over to me. He crouches down next to me. "Come on, love," he says, and gently pulls me to my feet.

He leads me out of the room and up the stairs to my bedroom, and my laughter gradually subsides into hiccups. Dad pulls back the covers on my bed and helps me into it before tucking me in. "Have a nap, sweetheart," he says gently. "Everything will be alright." He kisses me on the forehead then pulls my curtains closed. I snuggle down into the yin and yang duvet and close my eyes, my breath still shuddering between hiccups. Dad closes the door softly behind him as he leaves, and I soon fall fast asleep.

By the time I wake up, it's dark outside and I have a mouth like a sewer. Someone has left a glass of water on my bedside table and I gulp it down, then stagger to the bathroom to use the toilet and brush my teeth. Tentatively, I pad downstairs and discover that everyone has already left. All signs of the meal have been cleared away, and Mum and Dad are sitting there, staring at the television, but I can tell that they're not really watching it.

"Oh, darling!" Mum cries when she sees me, and I dive over to her and I snuggle into her open arms. Dad comes and sits next to us on the sofa and begins stroking my hair. I sniff and mumble an apology. Mum tuts and Dad says "Nonsense" and I let out a long, shaky sigh.

"What must everyone think of me?" I ask with my head buried against my mum's warm chest.

"Don't worry about that," Dad tells me firmly and Mum

squeezes me tighter.

"Are you still on your medication, love?" she asks gently. I nod. "Is it helping?"

"Yes," I lie.

"Come on, let's open the After Eights and watch a film," Dad suggests, and I nod and wipe my eyes.

The next day we set out on our traditional Boxing Day walk. We take Sammy, Mum and Dad's collie, and I throw his ball for him as we amble. He chases after it with boundless enthusiasm, retrieving it and returning it to me, panting eagerly, and I laugh as I pick up the drool-covered toy and toss it for the umpteenth time. The crisp air is invigorating, and I feel a sense of peace as we progress through the fields in our wellies. I can tell that Mum and Dad are happy to see me content, and I link arms with them as we watch Sammy go sniffing along a hedgerow. Vanessa is nowhere to be seen.

I spend the rest of the week learning to make origami flowers with Mum, helping Dad with his wine-making, polishing off the Christmas chocolates and reading a self-help book that I picked up at the train station. Apparently, I need to set myself some achievable goals and repeat positive mantras to myself, to change my mindset into a 'can-do' attitude. I've tried not to think too much about working on the pitch for Max Wild but I know I need to approach the challenge with less self-doubt, and reading this book is hopefully the first step in helping me to get there.

We don't talk about what happened on Christmas Day again, and for this I'm thankful. I don't really care what Margaret or Joy and Vernon think, but Arthur was a kind, sensible man, and I blush when I think about what he witnessed. I have no romantic interest in him, but he would be someone I would have enjoyed seeing again in normal circumstances. Oh well, *c'est la vie*.

Saturday is New Year's Eve, and we've been invited to a party at Mum's friend Brenda's house. As I get ready, Prince sings *1999* and Vanessa bops away on my shoulder. I wear a wine-red dress this time and leave my hair down around my shoulders. Dad whistles when he sees me coming down the stairs and I roll my eyes but smile. On my shoulder, Vanessa preens.

"You look lovely, darling," Mum tells me proudly.

"Not too thin?" I ask, patting my waist worriedly, and she tuts.

"Of course not."

Just then, the taxi arrives. Vanessa claps her hands in excitement and we go around switching off most of the lights before locking up. The driver is a talker, and we hear all about the argument he had with his brother-in-law over Christmas dinner. Cartoon steam blows out of his ears as he grows more and more irate, but it sounds to me like the brother-in-law was in the right (*Planes, Trains and Automobiles* is *definitely* better than *Home Alone*), so I refrain from commenting. Dad tells him in detail how such an argument would have been resolved in medieval times, and that shuts him up. I snort, and the driver gives me a strange look in the mirror. I get a tissue out of my clutch bag and blow my nose noisily.

Brenda lives on a sprawling farm with her husband, Bob. The taxi bumps up the long drive and the smell of manure assaults my nose as I climb out. All of the lights in the house are blazing and seventies music is pumping out through the open door. Currently, Wild Cherry are ordering white boys to *Play That Funky Music*. I brace myself for an evening of polite conversation with a bunch of my parents' generation. Hopefully, there will be gin.

Brenda screams and comes running, her blonde perm bouncing, when she sees my mum walk through the door and into the open-plan living area, and Mum screams back. They hug and air kiss, and Bob comes over and shakes Dad's hand. They look at their wives in exasperation, but I think it's quite sweet. They've known each other for donkey's years and they kept each other sane when they were young mums. Brenda is like a second mother to me. She turns to me next and with a "Hello, sweetheart!" she embraces me in a warm hug. She smells like vanilla and childhood.

We leave Mum chatting with her friend and Bob leads Dad and me over to the drinks table. There's a pink gin I haven't tried before and I go to pour myself a generous measure before catching Dad's worried glance and adjusting. ABBA sing *Mamma Mia, here we go again* in the background, and I give him a reassuring wink. He smiles and I can see the relief in his eyes. He turns to Bob and they start talking about the farm. I hang out next to them for a while, looking around at the other guests and waving to a few I recognise – mostly parents of kids I was at school with, plus a couple of Brenda's relatives that I've been introduced to over the years. I'm the only person in the room that's under fifty I realise as I bop subtly to the Bee Gees while they start breathing *Stayin' Alive*.

There's a buffet table, and after repeatedly casting it covetous glances for ten minutes, I give in and surreptitiously sidle over to it and sneak a mini sausage when no-one's looking. I'm starving. Before I know it, I'm grabbing another, then another. Soon my mouth is crammed with sausage and I'm struggling to chew, and of course that's when Tom Arnold walks into the room. My eyes bug and I chew rapidly, attempting to remove the evidence of my gluttony before he sees me. I swallow the last mouthful just as Marvin Gaye starts crooning *Let's Get It On* and Tom looks around and spots me. He blinks in surprise then smiles and waves. I raise my hand and smile back, closed-lipped in case I have sausage meat stuck between my teeth. Then someone taps his arm and the whole scene is ruined as I realise that he's here with a woman. He turns to her and Vanessa growls as we check out the stunning blonde with legs up to her armpits. I realise that I'm staring and pretend to look around the room while casting quick glances back at them. They're talking to Brenda, and I wonder how they know her and what on earth Tom is doing in this neck of the woods.

Mum spots me on my own and comes bustling over with a worried look on her face, and I reassure her that I'm fine. We start talking to one of Brenda's neighbours, who furtively reveals that my old headmistress has been having an affair with the vicar. Both of them are here, studiously ignoring each other at opposite ends of the room. As I imagine their secret liaisons, the stereo switches to Billy Paul's *Me and Mrs.*

Jones. I choke on my drink; believe it or not, her name actually *is* Mrs. Jones. Mum pats me on the back, and that's when Brenda announces that the buffet is open.

Chapter Seven

I find myself behind Tom in the queue for the food. We both reach for a vol-au-vent at the same time, and he does a double-take when he realises it's me. We exchange hellos and he introduces me to his girlfriend, Melanie. She smiles at me sweetly and reveals the cutest dimples I've ever seen. She's a primary school teacher, and annoyingly, I like her instantly. She's someone Lucy and I could be friends with.

"So, what's this one like to work with?" she asks with a teasing eye roll at Tom.

"Great!" I reply as Tom fidgets. "He's a fantastic boss."

"Pippa is going to be joining one of our creative teams after Christmas," he points out, trying to change the subject, and I purse my lips and narrow my eyes at him.

"He *bullied* me into it," I tell Melanie, and he opens his mouth to deny it.

"That sounds like Tom," Melanie says drily, and she elbows him in the ribs. "Once he gets his mind set on something, there's no stopping him. He's as stubborn as a mule."

"Speaking of which," Tom interjects, "how much did you

make for the donkey sanctuary in the end?"

"Over two hundred pounds," I reply, and he turns to Melanie.

"Pippa's amazing – she uses every opportunity to raise money for charity, from Bake Offs to pyjama days, you name it, she's done it." He looks at me proudly and I blush. I had no idea he knew about these events; he hasn't been at Mackay Lexington long enough to witness any except the 'Pounds for Kisses' for the donkeys. And no, reader, it didn't pass me by that he didn't mention the aforesaid kisses.

Melanie starts telling me about some of the fundraising events at her school, and as she talks I like her more and more, damn it. Why couldn't he have picked someone I could hate without a guilty conscience? There's no justice in the world.

You may be wondering what Vanessa has been up to this whole time and won't be surprised to hear that she's been sat on my shoulder sulking. *You've lost out to a better woman,* I think at her; *take it gracefully.* She thumbs her nose at me and I sigh.

Someone attracts Melanie's attention and she makes her apologies and turns away. Tom and I look at each other awkwardly and 10cc start singing *I'm Not In Love.* He turns red and clears his throat, pulling at his collar. "Is it me or is it hot in here?" he asks.

"It's you," I tell him, holding back a hysterical giggle as the song keeps playing. I decide to take pity on him. "So, how do you know Brenda and Bob?"

"My parents moved into the area a few months ago," he says with relief and gestures at a handsome couple who are talking to my dad and Bob. "What about you?"

"I grew up not too far away. Brenda and my mum go back ages."

"Ah. Which one's your mum?" I point her out. "Oh! The origami lady!"

"Oh no! Is that what she's known as now?" I cringe.

"Don't worry," he tells me in a stage whisper. "I won't tell anyone that *your* mother's the origami lady, if *you* don't reveal that *my* mother's known as the pole dancing lady." And I laugh out loud. He turns serious. "I hope I didn't really bully you into joining the team?" he asks earnestly.

"I would call it firm but gentle pressure rather than bullying," I tell him kindly, and he looks relieved.

"Melanie's right – once I set my sights on something, I find it hard not to go after it," he grimaces.

"It's probably why you're so good at your job. To be honest, I needed the push," I admit. I've decided that the New Year means a new me, and I'm going to stop holding myself back. My self-help book said to say yes to all new opportunities, and that's what I plan to do. Of course, I'm terrified, but what's the alternative? I can't go on the way I have been. It's time to stop playing it safe and believe in myself more.

Wow, this gin is good!

Melanie comes back, and they head off to re-join Tom's parents. I get collared by my old headmistress, and I can't help thinking that this would have been better as a 'Tarts and Vicars' party, but, again, that's someone else's story. I shake away an image of her dressed in a French maid's outfit, chasing the vicar around the parsonage with her feather duster, and listen politely as she tells me about the latest changes to the school curriculum. Vanessa starts nodding off on my shoulder and for a minute I wish I was as invisible as she is.

Mrs. Jones drones on for a good twenty minutes, needing only the occasional nod and 'Oh, really?' from me. I glance across to where Tom is and catch him staring at me, but he quickly looks away. Melanie noticed the look, and she gives me a small smile, which I return, but there's a little wrinkle between her brows as she turns back to Tom.

Fortunately, Brenda rescues me from Mrs. Jones, and escorts me over to the drinks table to re-fill my glass. We catch up on the latest family news and I love her even more when she doesn't ask me a single question about my love-life, God bless her. Mum and Dad join us, together with Bob, and I feel good about life as Sister Sledge start singing *We Are Family*. I link arms with Mum and Brenda and start swaying to the music. They join in and we start giggling. Dad winks at me and I look over at Tom and see him watching us with a soft smile on his face. He raises his glass to me and I grin. Melanie must have popped to the loo because I can't see her anywhere.

The song changes to *New York, New York* and Brenda grabs a few more friends who link arms with us, forming a longer chain. We start kicking our legs in time with the music, and soon all of the guests are joined in a circle, more than a few of them a little tipsy and off-balance. The chorus comes around and we join in at the tops of our lungs. Tom is laughing exuberantly opposite me, his whole face lit up, and I actually catch my breath at his beauty.

The song finishes, and we all clap and cheer. Melanie walks down the stairs and stops and blinks when she sees us all. I've got to admit, considering there are only the three of us under fifty in the room, I'm having a pretty decent time.

Brenda decides it's time for a few party games, and I find myself having to pass a balloon between my body and Tom's without using my hands. I discover that he's uber-competitive and he coaches me through the manoeuvrings like it's a professional team sport. We manage it expertly and he turns to pass it on to Melanie, but she can't seem to follow his instructions as well. She drops the balloon and it has to go back to the beginning of the line, but manages it on the second pass and our team is victorious. Tom high fives Melanie and me and I feel like a million dollars.

The next game is the Suck and Blow game, and we have to pass a playing card down the line using only our lips. I try to sit out of this one but the teams would be left uneven so I'm roped back in. Vanessa sniggers as she notices Mrs. Jones wrangle a position next to the vicar.

Brenda plays Prince's *Kiss* and the game begins. As the card moves up the line, with a few comedy re-starts, I prepare myself to suck as hard as possible. My turn arrives, and I take it with ease from the woman before me and keep sucking as I quickly turn around to Tom. But something goes wrong as I pass it onto his lips. I think he has it so I stop sucking, but the card drops and his lips land on mine. Vanessa claps and squeals, while I blink in surprise and bend to pick up the card, my face red, then hurriedly pass it back to the start of the line. Tom doesn't say anything to me as the card starts working its way along the line again but I see him studying my face before I turn away. This time when it gets to us the transition goes smoothly and he manages to pass it onto Melanie with no problem. Again, our team triumphs, but this time I scamper away before the high fives commence.

I head to the drinks table and pour myself another gin – my last, I promise myself. Mum comes over to check on me. She's a little tipsy herself and she giggles as she tells me that she thinks my dad dropped the card on purpose. I roll my eyes but smile, and wonder if Tom did the same. The thought makes me uncomfortable, what with his (lovely) girlfriend being there and all.

I turn and find him behind me, looking apologetic, and I find it hard to make eye contact. He clears his throat.

"Sorry about that – I think I've had a little too much to drink and my timing was off," he tells me, grimacing.

"Oh! Don't worry about it. Same here," I reply awkwardly. He nods stiffly, and busies himself getting fresh drinks for himself and Melanie before taking his leave and heading back over to her. She looks a bit disgruntled, and I cringe inwardly. Nazareth starts singing *Love Hurts* and I knock my gin back in one. Brenda hurries to put something livelier on.

Midnight soon looms and we gather in a circle and cross our arms and hold hands as we count down to a chorus of 'Happy New Year!' We start singing *Auld Lang Syne* and I hear fireworks going off in the distance. People turn to each other and wish each other 'Happy New Year', exchanging kisses and handshakes. I'm soon confronted with Tom and I offer him my cheek, which he pecks chastely, before I turn to Melanie and give her a hug. She returns my murmured 'Happy New Year' sweetly and then we each turn to the next person.

After all the exchanges are done, things mellow, and everyone sits around drinking and waxing lyrical about their hopes for the coming year. I've learned not to make resolutions, but I aim to make the most of new opportunities like my self-help book suggests, starting with the pitch for Max Wild. I look over at Tom, and he's giving Melanie his full attention, as if making up for his earlier lapses. I must admit to a twinge of jealousy, which I quickly squash. I really do wish them well. Vanessa has fallen asleep again, and doesn't notice the lack of attention.

By one o'clock, most of the guests are leaving. Our cab is booked for half past, and we sit around with Brenda and Bob and the last few guests, chatting. Tom and Melanie have already left, with a wave from across the room, and I start nodding off in the armchair, a little bit of drool coming out the corner of my mouth.

Dad nudges me awake when the taxi arrives and we hug our friends goodbye and head home. I feel a strange mixture of happiness and sadness as the movement of the car rocks me back into quasi-sleep, and I pray to whoever's up there that good things lie in wait for me in the coming year.

I head back to London in the late afternoon of New Year's Day. This time, my reserved seat is empty and I sit in it smugly, watching the train fill up and disgruntled passengers tutting as they board to find that *their* seat is taken. The Monkees sing *Last Train to Clarksville* and I nod along, feeling good about the New Year.

To my surprise, Lucy is waiting at the station when I arrive. I blink when I see Miranda next to her, but smile when I see that they're both grinning widely, their faces flushed with happiness. I hug them both, and arch my eyebrow at Lucy. "Sorted?" I ask, and she nods and blushes, holding out her left hand to me. There's a diamond on her ring finger, and I squeal and grab her in a bear hug when the penny drops. Miranda gets the same treatment, and her cork-screw curls end up in my face, almost smothering me, but I don't mind – I'm too happy for them. "Tell me everything!" I demand, and Lucy starts gushing the story, while Miranda's beautiful brown skin pinkens even further, though she beams proudly at her fiancée.

"So," Lucy begins, "remember when I told you that Miranda had said that she was working late, and I saw her with Phoebe in that restaurant?" I nod. "Well, it turns out that she'd asked Phoebe to help her pick out an engagement ring, and they were just grabbing a bite to eat first!"

"Oh my God!"

"I know! The whole thing was just one big misunderstanding."

"It will teach you not to jump to conclusions," Miranda scolds her gently, and Lucy grimaces. But they look so lovingly into each other's eyes that it's clear that all is forgiven.

"I did try to tell her to give you chance to explain," I tell Miranda.

"I know you did," she says, patting my arm. "She's a stubborn madam." She winks at Lucy, who rolls her eyes and chuckles sheepishly.

"Miranda got fed up with me not answering her calls, so she turned up at my brother's house on Christmas Day, and persuaded me to go for a walk with her. I told her what I'd seen and she explained everything, then got down on one knee and proposed," she sighs, and her eyes glow at the memory. Miranda pulls her in for a kiss, and I cheer.

We decide to head out for a meal to celebrate, dropping my bag off along the way. We end up at a small Italian restaurant not far from my flat, complete with red-and-white chequered table cloths, and gorge ourselves on pasta and garlic ciabatta. They're already discussing plans for the wedding, hoping for one in the late spring or early summer, and we chat non-stop about colour schemes, flowers and the guest list.

"We've got something to ask you," Lucy says halfway through the meal. They look at each other, and Miranda nods with a wink.

"Well?" I say in the pause. "Don't keep me in suspense!"

Lucy takes a breath.-"Will you be our bridesmaid? We'll understand if it's too much for you," she adds quickly, looking worried.

"Oh! Of course I will – it will be an honour!" I tell her, clapping my hands in excitement, and they squeal. I rush to stretch over the table and hug them, and we laugh and jump back as the bottle of wine topples over. The waiter comes over to clean up the mess. When he's done, I order a bottle of champagne and we toast to their engagement.

It's late when we head home. Lucy has already collected her things from my flat and moved back into the one she shares with Miranda, so we part ways at the end of my road, hugging each other one last time as I murmur, "Congratulations, my lovelies – I'm so damn happy for you!" They head off, arms linked, and I sigh as I watch them go. Al Green sings *Let's Stay Together* and all's well in the world.

Chapter Eight

I have a slight headache the next morning but two glasses of water and a couple of paracetamol do their magic, and it's receded by the time I arrive at work. The temp booked to replace me on reception for the next few months turns up shortly afterwards and I spend half an hour talking her through the phone system and general procedures before taking a deep breath and reporting to Tom.

He smiles as he looks up and sees me at his door, and gestures for me to enter and sit down.

"Everything okay with the temp?"

"Yes, she seems to know what she's doing," I tell him. "Her name's Jean and she has a lot of experience."

"Good." He claps his hands together. "I've decided to head up the creative team on the Wild Spirit account as it's such a big one. The first meeting to brainstorm initial thoughts is at ten in Conference Room 2. I've got a brief from Max and he's coming in later in the week to see if we're on the right track. He wants to be as hands-on as possible. You can use the desk next to Evie's, and –" he looks at me seriously, but there's a little twinkle in his eye "—if you do well on this, it could be yours permanently; that's if it's something that you would want."

I blink and my heart starts pounding. I nod jerkily, my mouth suddenly too dry to speak. He chuckles. "Max seemed really impressed with what he saw, and he's notoriously hard to please. I'm looking forward to seeing what you come up with."

No pressure, Pip!

I collect a few things from reception, where Jean's working the phone, and head to my new desk in the open-plan office. I spend the time before the meeting arranging my things and chatting to Evie, whose desk is intimidatingly immaculate. Lucy is on the phone not far away and she gives me a thumbs up, and Tim waves from across the other side of the room. On the other side of Evie is Mike, who has the untidiest desk I've ever seen, with numerous cans of fizzy drinks dotted haphazardly over the surface and crisp packets scattered around the bin. Stan and Llewellyn's desks are opposite. They all greet me cheerfully, and I soon feel comfortable to be there and less like an imposter.

Ten o'clock arrives and I take a notepad and pen with me and head to the conference room. It's already half full when I enter. I take a seat quietly, place my things on the table in front of me, and wipe my sweaty hands down my skirt. In the room are a range of experts in their field – from graphic designers to copywriters, editors, artists and web developers. I gulp as I realise how out of my depth I am, and feel my hands start to shake.

Tom is the last to walk in and everyone settles down as he

makes his way to his seat. The table is already littered with coffee mugs and glasses of water, notepads and pens, and some people have already rolled their sleeves up. I take a deep breath and that's when Tom catches my eye and winks. I smile back and feel myself relax a little while Tom welcomes everyone and introduces the brief and budget. He stresses the importance of landing Wild Spirit Inc. as a client and talks inspiringly about how this needs to be the best pitch we've ever presented. People nod seriously and most are already taking notes, including me. In fact, I find myself writing down verbatim every word that Tom's saying and I force myself to make shorter notes and only write down what's relevant. I feel like a student starting uni for the first time again.

To my surprise, Tom then welcomes me to the team and explains that I have an art degree and how Max Wild spotted my secret talent. Everyone looks at me curiously and I blush. *Don't get your hopes up*, I plead silently, but Tom's next words ease the pressure dramatically.

"I want Pippa to be treated like an intern, or an apprentice," he begins. "She's largely going to be working with the art team, coming up with ideas and storyboards, but I'd like her to grow familiar with what each section does, and how the whole process works – how we move from initial ideas to a holistic ad campaign. I'm sure you'll all make her welcome." More nods and several smiles, and I blow out a little breath and smile gratefully in return.

Tom asks for initial ideas, and a few people share their thoughts. There's a buzz in the room as the discussion builds, and I feel a surge of excitement. My fingers itch to start sketching, and I begin doodling on my pad as people talk about scenarios and slogans, image, tone and audience. Brand awareness stats and market research gets presented, and this prompts the discussion to go in a new direction. I sketch and sketch, and I see other people doing the same on their pads.

After a couple of hours or so, the room is starting to smell like sweat and stale coffee, and Tom brings the meeting to an end and tells everyone to go and get lunch. A vision has been created and we all have a clear brief to follow. Simon, who's the head artist, asks me to join him and a couple of others for lunch and we get to know each other better over paninis and tomato salads at a local café.

We spend the afternoon storyboarding our ideas, but nothing stands out yet as being the perfect fit. Simon tells me that this is normal, and not to worry. He tells me to just keep sketching and a spark will happen. I feel so motivated that I stay late, not heading home until after seven. Even then I feel invigorated rather than tired, and as I sit on the bus trundling closer to home, thought bubbles pop up around my head with tens of possible storylines inside. I rub out the things I want to improve and edit repeatedly, the bubbles popping and popping in the air as the ideas develop and change rapidly.

It's only when I get to my front door and put the key in the lock that I realise that I've had a full day without Vanessa appearing, not once. It's the first time in two years that I've been without her for so long and it feels strange. I kind of miss her, now that I'm on my own, but at least it meant that I had no distractions on my first day on the team. I haven't heard a single song either; my mind has been unusually settled. I guess Dad is right – it's good to keep busy. Don't get me wrong, it can be quite good fun when a song bursts into your head to suit the occasion, and Vanessa, though a complete slut, can be rather entertaining, but I *know* it's not normal. I'm not *completely* deranged. I prefer the word 'quirky' anyway.

I enter my flat, and hang my bag and coat up, then head to the freezer and pop a frozen meal into the microwave. I used to cook more, but it seems pointless going to all that effort for one person. I grab a glass of water and head to the small breakfast bar with my sketch pad, where I keep doodling until the microwave pings, and even after, as I sit forking the cheesy lasagne into my mouth, blowing it to cool each mouthful, I sit sketching between bites.

It's after eleven when I finally call it a night and get ready for bed. I fall asleep dreaming of story boards and jingles.

The next few days pass in a blur of creativity. The art team meets regularly and we bounce ideas off each other, improving and dismissing concept after concept. Tom catches up with us regularly, making sure that we're keeping to brief, and I spend time with the other sections of the team, getting a crash course in advertising as I watch them work on other campaigns and prepare for the Wild Spirit campaign.

Max is due in tomorrow; Tom wants us to select our five best concepts to share where we're at. One of the ideas that Simon selects is an original of mine, and I feel proud as he adds the draft storyboards to the selection. It's a sequence that starts in black and white, with only the red of a young woman's umbrella picked out in colour. She waits in the rain outside a restaurant, and a love story unfolds. It's less about the specific product, and more about the Wild Spirit brand as a whole, so it's a risk, but Simon says it's good to pitch at least one idea that's a bit outside of the box.

"Having fresh eyes on the team is doing us a world of good," he reassures me, and I feel myself redden with embarrassment and pleasure.

Of course, Vanessa *would* choose the day that Max Wild is due to reappear. I lay awake worrying all night and so I slept through my alarm. She lounges on my dressing table while I bustle around getting ready, making a quick call to work to let them know I'm running late. I skip breakfast and she sits on my shoulder as I hurry to the bus stop. I sit biting my nails for the whole journey, my foot twitching, while Vanessa makes eyes at a student across the aisle. The meeting is due to start at half nine.

It's nine-forty when I enter the building and rush into the lift. I jab at the button repeatedly when it doesn't respond within a micro-second and get an odd look from the other occupant. The doors finally close and the lift starts ascending at a snail's pace. I tap my foot and glare at the doors, my arms folded tightly, and the man warily moves further away from me.

At last, we reach the right floor and I lunge out of the lift as the doors creep apart, squeezing myself through the gap before they're fully open. I don't have time to check my appearance in the mirror in the loos, so I just hurry to the conference room, keeping my fingers crossed that I don't look too dishevelled.

I get to the door and everyone looks up as I barge in and go flying over the threshold. I land flat on my face and people rush out of their seats to pick me up. "I'm fine! I'm fine!" I tell them, my face red as I'm hauled up by my arms. I look up and see Tom and Max staring at me with open mouths from across the other side of the table, and that's when Simon murmurs in my ear that my skirt is tucked into my knickers. "Shit!" I hiss, and reach round to pull it out. I must have done the whole journey here with my love heart pants on display.

I hear a masculine chuckle, and look up quickly to see Max twinkling those blue eyes at me. Tom joins in and so do a few others. I finally see the funny side too and grin, and the tension is broken.

I raise my hands. "I'm so sorry everyone – is there any way I can start this day all over again?"

I receive more chuckles and sympathetic glances as Simon pulls out a chair for me and Max pours me a coffee. Things settle down and the meeting re-starts. Tom is in the middle of summarising our progress so far and after a few minutes he hands over to Simon, who presents the storyboards for the five ideas that were selected. Max looks over them all and asks a few questions about each, which Simon answers confidently. I see his eyes linger on my idea with a thoughtful look in them, and I hold my breath.

"What's the idea behind this one?" he finally asks when the others have been discussed, and Simon explains that it's the wild card, encompassing the brand as a whole.

"That wasn't in the brief."

"We like to offer something outside the box, as well as

proposals that directly address the client's brief – sometimes it can take a campaign in a new, fresh direction. The results can be surprising yet rewarding," Tom interjects. He winks at me, but Max doesn't notice as he's busy examining the storyboards and digesting his words.

"I like it," he finally says, and I release the breath I hadn't realised I'd been holding. "It's not right for *this* campaign but we could definitely use it in another, further down the line." He looks up. "Whose idea was this?"

"Pippa's," Simon tells him proudly. I blush and murmur something about the team effort. Max looks at me intensely, and I see Tom glance at him sharply.

They look back at the other four proposals, and Max eventually chooses the one that he'd like us to focus on. He has a few suggestions for changes, and we all take notes. When it's clear that the meeting is drawing to an end, Tom thanks everyone for their hard work and we start filing out. I stop when I hear my name called, though. "Just a minute, Pippa," Tom says, and I linger awkwardly at the side of the door as everyone exits. Tom and Max keep talking on the other side of the large desk until only the three of us are left.

Finally, they turn back to me. "Pippa," Max begins, "I just wanted to say well done for what you've produced. It seems I discovered a hidden gem."

"You certainly did," Tom tells him mildly, but there's a hooded look in his eyes that I can't quite work out ... competitiveness?

"What made you go off in such a different direction from the brief, though?" Max asks curiously.

"I, erm, was just trying to see the big picture, I suppose," I answer uncertainly. To be honest, I don't know where I get my ideas from; this one just popped into my head, like a lightbulb moment.

He nods at me approvingly. "Well, keep up the good work." He turns to Tom. "Keep Pippa's idea on the back burner for now. Let's get the campaign for the flavoured vodka up and running, and then if I'm happy with that – and I like what I've seen so far – we'll come back to it." They shake hands, and Max asks me to accompany him to the lift. I see Tom narrow his eyes as Max places his hand on my lower back and guides me out of the room.

Max doesn't speak until we get to the lift and he pushes the button for the ground floor. Then, while we're waiting, he turns to me. "What are you doing on Saturday night?" he asks me bluntly. I blink and flush, then look back to where Tom's watching us, making no pretence at hiding it.

I turn back. "I – erm …"

"I'd like to discuss your proposal in more detail," he continues, and I relax a bit. "We might as well do it over dinner – we've both got to eat." He looks me up and down with a concerned frown, and it's clear that he thinks I'm a bit on the skinny side. I do eat – you must have seen enough evidence of that by now, reader – but a couple of years ago my weight plummeted, and I haven't been able to put it back on.

I murmur my acceptance of his invitation and he asks for my address, telling me he'll pick me up at seven, then the lift arrives and he's saying goodbye. We maintain eye contact as the doors close, then he's gone.

I turn to find Tom is still there. He raises an eyebrow and I hurry over and tell him quickly about the dinner meeting. He doesn't look too happy about it, and I suppose it *is* a bit unconventional, but I could hardly refuse such a huge potential client, and I think Tom realises this. He nods stiffly and I head over to Simon's desk to start working on Max's changes.

I meet up with Tim and Lucy for lunch and regale them with the horror story that was my morning (minus Max's invitation). They think it's hilarious and can't stop laughing about it for a good twenty minutes. Finally, they calm down and Tim announces that he's met someone new (again). This one's called Lola (cue The Kinks). I ask if she drinks champagne that tastes like cola and Lucy snorts, but the joke goes over Tim's head.

"She's twenty-five. She has –" *a dark brown voice* "– red hair and she –" *walks like a woman but talks like a man* "– works in publishing and she –" *picked me up and sat me on her knee* "– likes reading and cycling," he beams.

"She sounds … great!" I tell him. He lost me at cycling. I tried cycling to work once but had to swerve to avoid bumping into someone who was on the wrong side of the road. I ended up in a holly bush and didn't see the irony when I shouted, "Prick!" at the top of my voice.

"Where did you meet her?" Lucy asks.

"In a book shop," he responds enthusiastically. "We both reached for *Men Are from Mars, Women Are from Venus* at the same time. Isn't that funny?"

"Hilarious," I tell him.

"I think this is the one," he says, and Lucy groans. "I *mean* it this time – there's this *spark* between us," he insists. "She's like, the perfect woman."

"There's no such thing as the perfect woman," Lucy tells him. "In fact, the more perfect she seems on the surface, the darker and weirder her kinks probably are." I snort and Lucy high-fives me. Tim looks at us in confusion.

I take pity on him. "Just remember to be *cool* but not *too* cool this time," I say gently.

He nods seriously. "Right, right – find the right balance."

"Mmm … gentlemanly, but not *smothering*," I tell him.

"Pay the bill, but *don't* buy her a present on the first date," Lucy adds.

"Offer to walk her home, but don't talk about how you'd furnish your first *house* together," I warn.

"Ask her questions, but don't ask what she would name your *children*," Lucy finishes.

The whole time, Tim is nodding earnestly. "Great! What can go wrong?" he asks, and I hold back a grimace.

Chapter Nine

I fall into a routine at work. There's a lot to learn, but the team is so helpful I don't feel overwhelmed. They all treat me as if I deserve to be there, and I feel less and less like an imposter as the week goes on. Even Lisa's started treating me with more respect now I'm not 'just' the receptionist.

Vanessa appears less and less during work hours, and is a lot quieter, though she still smoulders when she *is* around and sees Tom, who takes the time to check in on me regularly.

On Friday, he makes a point of stopping at my desk just before home time. He makes a show of looking over my work, but I can tell there's something else on his mind. He lingers, drumming his fingers on the surface, and when Simon moves away, he quietly asks me if I'm still meeting Max tomorrow. I nod – he'd called me that morning to confirm; Jean had transferred him through to me and we'd had a short but pleasant conversation. Tom nods and opens his mouth as if to say something, but thinks better of it and slaps his hand down on the table with a 'Have fun!' before hesitating, then walking away.

I start tidying my desk, wondering what all that was about,

but I'm soon distracted by mentally sifting through my wardrobe, trying to decide what to wear to the (date?) meeting. Clothes flash across a rack in front of me, and I stop at both the Little Black Dress that I wore to the Christmas Do and the wine-red dress that I wore on New Year's Eve. I dismiss both and continue searching, finally stopping at an emerald knee-length dress with three-quarter sleeves and a love-heart neck line.

My musing is interrupted by Simon. "See you Monday – great work this week!" he says as he heads to the lift, and I smile and wave in acknowledgement then start gathering my things. Evie grabs me for a quick chat and then I'm heading home myself, with butterflies in my tummy as I think about tomorrow night.

I'm up bright and early on Saturday, giving the flat a brisk clean before I shower and head to the supermarket (those frozen meals and bottles of wine won't buy themselves, reader!). The shop is rammed and I silently fume at the people who leave their trolley in the middle of the aisle as they go hunting on the shelves for half an hour. I imagine forcefully shoving one of the trolleys away and it goes careening down the aisle knocking all the offenders out of the way like skittles, while everyone else claps and cheers. Of course, I don't – I tut loudly and gently move their trolley over by two inches as I squeeze my way around it.

The queues are massive, and I while away the time listening to The Clash singing *Lost in The Supermarket*, bopping my head and tapping my foot in time to the music as we creep forwards. Finally, I'm served, and of course, I brightly tell the lady on the check-out that it's "No problem at all!" when she apologises for keeping me waiting.

I head home and unpack the shopping, before making an omelette and salad for lunch, then I spend the afternoon trying to read *Jane Eyre* for the hundred and eighty-seventh time without checking my watch every two minutes.

Mum calls in the late afternoon, and this fills half an hour. She has a new hobby – palm reading. She's bought a book, and practises on the old folk in the home where she volunteers. She promises to do mine when she sees me and I grimace but tell her that it sounds like a wonderful idea.

At five o' clock, I decide to get ready. I take another shower and spend a long time trying to put my hair up into an elegant chignon, cursing myself for not booking in at the salon. Vanessa huffs at me impatiently and I rudely tell her to shut up. Finally, it's in some semblance of a style, and I finish getting ready, though I have to do my mascara twice because I sneeze before the first application is dry and it smears under my eyes.

I'm ready by six-thirty. I know it's not really a *date* date, but this is the first time I've been out with a man in more than two years and I can't help feeling nervous. It doesn't help that he looks like a cross between Robert Redford and Bradley Cooper either. As this thought crosses my mind, Vanessa *Mmms* in appreciation and I swat at her. "No funny business tonight, madam," I tell her, and she pouts.

The minutes hand ticks steadily on, and just before seven the door buzzer finally rings. I hurry over to the intercom and tell Max I'll be down in a minute before grabbing my clutch bag and flicking off most of the lights. I scurry down the stairs and my damn heel twists again, but I make it to the door in one piece. I open it and breathe "Hi!" and Max smiles at me appreciatively as he looks me over and kisses me on the cheek. He smells like spicy aftershave and heaven.

"Shall we?" He offers me his arm and leads me over to his limo where a driver is waiting by the open door. My eyes bug and Max chuckles and helps me in. I feel like Cinderella, or Julia Roberts in *Pretty Woman*. Vanessa is loving it.

We settle into the plush seats and Max offers me a glass of champagne which I accept politely, but my hand is shaking as I reach for the glass.

"So, tell me a bit about yourself, Pippa," Max says as the car starts moving and he relaxes back in his seat. I feel like I'm in a job interview. I sit up straight and try to answer professionally.

"Well, I came to London to attend university and decided to stay. I've been a receptionist at Mackay Lexington for three years and before that I did a few other admin jobs ..." I trail off as I notice him frowning and shaking his head.

"No. Tell me about *you*, not your CV," he demands, and I gulp.

"Me?" I squeak. I clear my throat. "What do you want to know?" I ask weakly. "That I like walks in the rain and cosy nights in?" I attempt to joke, but he just frowns harder.

"If that's the truth."

"I prefer walks in the sunshine."

"But you *do* like cosy nights in?"

"Sometimes."

"What do you do for fun?"

"I … I see friends, I read, I draw … what about you?"

"We can get to me later," he says dismissively, and I take a large sip of my champagne.

"What do you like to read?"

"I like the Brontës and Jane Austen."

"What did you study at university?"

"Art."

"Of course. Have you ever been married?"

I hesitate. "Yes."

He opens his mouth as if to pursue that further but notices the look on my face and appears to change his mind.

"Do you have a good relationship with your parents?"

"I do," I say with relief.

"Tell me about them."

I take a deep breath. "My dad's a history lecturer and my mum volunteers at a home for the elderly – and has a *lot* of hobbies."

"What sort of hobbies?" he asks curiously, and I tell him. He chuckles at my vivid descriptions of a house full of wonky pottery, abstract portraits, unfinished erotica novels, origami animals (not forgetting Yoda and Darth Vader) and my dread of getting my palm read. I feel myself relaxing more and more as the conversation centres away from me so I venture to ask *him* another question.

"Do *you* have any hobbies?" I ask tentatively.

He must be satisfied with his grilling of me because he crosses his ankle on his knee and seems happy to talk about himself at last. "I enjoy skiing and horse riding – and I'm taking flying lessons."

"Very outdoorsy."

He nods. "I like to be active." I grimace. "Don't you?"

I tell him about my attempts at yoga and cycling, and about the time I tried indoor rock climbing with Lucy and landed heavily on my butt as I let the rope out too fast – I couldn't sit down comfortably for a week afterwards. He watches me in fascination as I speak, and I realise that I must be completely different from the sort of women that he's used to spending time with. Perhaps I'm a novelty for him – that might explain his interest in me.

The limo arrives at one of the swankiest restaurants in town and the driver comes around and opens the door for us. Max holds my hand as he helps me out of the vehicle and doesn't let it go as we move into the restaurant. He's greeted familiarly and respectfully by the *maitre d'* and we're led to a table in a cosy corner where Max studies the wine menu and asks if I have any preference. Of course, I don't, so he orders for us.

While I'm studying the food menu, I sense him watching me and I wonder what he's thinking. I look up and the little wrinkle between his brows disappears as he smiles.

"Are you trying to figure me out?" I ask archly, and he chuckles.

"Sorry. I make it my business to get to know the people I

surround myself with inside and out. It's what makes a good manager."

"Ah."

"I haven't quite worked *you* out yet though."

"Oh, I'm quite simple really," I tell him lightly.

"I don't think you are," he frowns.

The waiter comes back with the wine, which Max tastes and approves, then we order our food, and I'm relieved when he's gone and Max decides to change the subject.

"So, how have you settled into the creative team? I imagine it's quite a bit different from working reception?"

"I'm loving it. Everyone's been so helpful. Actually, I wanted to thank you for creating this opportunity for me – I never would have had the confidence to put myself out there on my own," I tell him earnestly, and I realise that I've placed my hand over his and go to pull it back, but he catches hold of it and doesn't let go.

"You're welcome," he says softly, holding my gaze. "But your talent really spoke for itself. I'm surprised no one else spotted it earlier."

"Oh, I kept my art work hidden," I tell him flippantly.

"Why?" he asks with an intense frown.

I shrug. "Lack of confidence I guess."

"Why would someone like you lack confidence?"

I squirm and he takes pity on me. "Tell me about your vision for the storyboards you created." He sits back, and I start chattering away in relief, barely pausing for breath. I tell him about my idea for a whole series of ads, which follow the same couple in a 'will they, won't they?' storyline, and I feel my face light up with enthusiasm. The food arrives, and Max asks me more questions about brand awareness and product placement, and we discuss the possibilities as we eat the sumptuous meal. I relax more and more as the wine bottle empties and the conversation goes on. We bounce ideas off each other, and I can see that Max is excited by the prospect of such a big campaign.

"It won't be cheap," he finally tells me.

"You can afford it," I tell him with a wink, spooning my dessert into my mouth, and he chuckles at my cheek.

"I think I've created a monster."

"You may very well have."

He leans forward. "An adorable monster, though." And I smile and blush. "Can I see you again?" he asks abruptly.

"You'll see me at work," I tease.

"You know what I mean, madam." His blue eyes twinkle, and Vanessa trembles with excitement. I take a sip of my wine, pretending to think, and he narrows his eyes at me playfully.

"I suppose so," I finally tell him, and he grins.

"Good! You had me worried for a minute there."

I tut. "I think you must be far too used to getting your own way."

He grimaces. "How do you know me so well already?"

"While you've been figuring *me* out, I've been figuring *you* out," I tell him archly.

"Have you now? And what else have you 'figured out'?"

"You like to be in control."

"There aren't many people in my position who don't."

"But you like it so much you won't even drink more than one glass of wine."

"You noticed that?"

"Mmm."

"You *are* observant."

"It's the artist in me," I tell him, then blurt out, "I'd like to draw you some time." I clap my hand over my mouth, an appalled expression on my face.

"Would you?" he asks, surprised. "I'm not very good at sitting still for long."

"Forget I said anything."

"No, no – let's do it. I've never sat for my portrait before. It will be an experience. I'm away on business in the Far East for a couple of weeks, but we can get together when I get back … maybe on the first Saturday after I return you can come to my place and I'll sit for you. I'll even throw lunch in, how does that sound?"

I gulp and nod. We exchange phone numbers and I look around and realise that we're one of the last set of diners left. We've been here for hours.

Max thanks the *maitre d'* as we put our coats on and head out to the waiting limo. He holds my hand on the seat between us as the vehicle heads back to my flat. He asks me softly about my husband, and I tell him quietly, and he strokes his thumb over my finger. "I'm sorry," he says when I finish, and I shrug.

"It happens every day."

"But it happened to you."

I nod, and the limo pulls up in front of my building. The driver opens the door for us and Max walks me to the door. He leans over and kisses me gently on the mouth. "I'll see you in a couple of weeks," he murmurs, and I smile at him shyly before turning to put the key in the lock. He stays until I'm inside, then walks away. I close the door softly and lean back against it, releasing a long breath. Then, smiling to myself, I head up the stairs to get ready for bed.

Chapter Ten

On Sunday, Mum and Dad get the train down and take me out to lunch. They usually do this once a month or so, but I think my Christmas Day breakdown worried them and they've come a bit sooner to check up on me. I greet them at the station at twelve o'clock, and lead them to a pub that does a good carvery not too far away. They ask me how my new role at work is going, and I tell them how fulfilling it is and how much busier I am. I don't tell them about my date with Max.

Dad is pleased I'm busy and Mum is glad that I'm using my talent as more than a hobby. This prompts me (reluctantly) to ask about *her* latest interest and she starts gushing about 'Mounts of Mercury' and 'Head Lines'. She promises to read my palm before they head back and I grimace at Dad, who winks at me. I know he appreciates it when I indulge her, and I don't want to crush her enthusiasm, so I brace myself for what's to come.

We tuck into our roast dinners and Dad launches into a history of fortune-telling through the ages, and that keeps the conversation going until dessert. Indulgently, we order sticky toffee puddings with custard, and while we're waiting for them to arrive, Mum decides it's time. She holds my hand in front of her and frowns seriously down at it for some minutes. She tuts once and I raise my eyebrows at Dad, who smiles.

"Has she read your palm?" I ask him, and he nods. "What did she discover?"

"That I'm stubborn, curious and easily distracted."

"I could have told you that."

"And I'm going to live a long life and have only one love." I smirk at this.

"Shhh!" Mum tells us, and I put on my most serious face.

"Hmm," she says at last. "Well, you have a Water Hand – that means that you're sensitive and imaginative. Very creative."

"Well, that's a surprise," I say drily as Vanessa leans over my shoulder curiously.

Mum carries on as if I haven't spoken. "Your Head Line has a break in it, possibly signifying mental strife, but your Mount of Saturn reveals great fortitude."

I sigh, but Mum ignores me. Dad winks at me again. "You have a long life line, which is good, and your heart line is forked, which means –"

"Okay – I get the general idea," I interrupt rudely, and Mum purses her lips but lets my hand go when I pull it back. Dad frowns at me but doesn't say anything and I quickly jump up and brightly ask if anyone wants another drink before scampering off to the bar.

After we've finished our desserts, we head to the park for

a walk. I link arms with Mum and ask her loads of questions about her other hobbies and the clubs that she attends to make up for my earlier abruptness, and I can tell that I'm forgiven.

Their return train is at four, so at half past three we start walking back to the station. I ask how Arthur is and Dad says he's well and that he'd asked after me. I tell him to say 'Hi' from me and he promises that he will.

The train is already waiting when we arrive and we kiss goodbye on the platform with a 'See you next month!' Dad tells me not to hang around in the cold once they've boarded so I wave to them through the window as they find their seats, then head home to Mr. Fluffles and a stack of ironing.

Tom calls me into his office on Monday morning and asks me bluntly how the 'meeting' went. He says it with the inverted commas clear in his tone. I frown and squirm uncomfortably but he doesn't notice. He seems to have gotten out of bed on the wrong side judging by the way he's been storming around the office grunting at everyone since he arrived. I've never seen him like this before and I don't quite know how to handle him. I open my mouth to answer but close it again, and he finally seems to realise how rude he's being.

His gaze softens. "Did it go well?" he asks in a gentler voice. I nod and tell him about the ideas we came up with for a series of ads with a progressive storyline.

"That's brilliant!" he tells me, his eyes lighting up, and I feel my cheeks turn pink at the praise. "Do you have the time to storyboard initial ideas for the series while working with

Simon on the campaign for the vodka? The more we can show Max now, the more likely he is to start a long-term relationship with us."

I tell him I can fit it in and he claps his hands together, pleased. I feel duty-bound to inform him that I'm seeing Max again when he returns from his business trip.

"To discuss the idea further?" he asks in surprise.

I shift uncomfortably in my chair, and finally admit that I'm doing his portrait.

"Oh." The light in his eyes diminishes, and the grump is back. He starts shuffling the papers on his desk. "Well, just keep it professional, okay?" he snaps, and I inhale sharply.

He turns red and avoids eye-contact. I stand stiffly and he opens his mouth as if to say something, then snaps it closed stubbornly. I leave the room and make a point of shutting the door softly but in my head I slam it and the glass wall shatters. The Beastie Boys sing *Fight For Your Right* and I stomp back to my desk where I begin sketching furiously. Simon heads towards me with some storyboards, then raises his hands and veers away as I look up and he sees the scowl on my face. Vanessa sulks on my shoulder because one of her dreamboats isn't happy with us, but I ignore her and sit muttering to myself about bears with sore heads.

"Talking to yourself is the first sign of madness," Lucy's voice pipes up beside me, and I look up to see her arching her eyebrow and twinkling her eyes at me.

"I'm well past the first sign," I tell her.

"We all are," she replies flippantly, popping herself onto

my desk. "Life would be boring if we were all 'normal'." She wiggles her fingers in the air to make inverted commas.

"To what do I owe the pleasure anyway?" I ask curiously. Lucy's normally too busy to spend much time stopping by for a chat during work hours.

"Just checking you're available for lunch today?" she responds innocently, but there's a look in her eyes that suggests she's got an agenda.

"Sure," I tell her. "Shall I ask Tim?"

"Already done." She hops off the desk. "See you at one." And with that she's gone. I stare after her, wondering what that was all about. I guess I'll find out at lunch time. At least it's a distraction from stewing over my encounter with Tom, the grouch-bag.

The morning passes unpleasantly. There's a tense atmosphere and everyone who comes out of Tom's office does so grimacing, so most people avoid going in. When he needs to speak to someone, he opens the door and barks their name and they go running. I keep my head down and I'm relieved when one o'clock arrives and I haven't been summoned again.

Lucy and Tim are waiting at the lift for me. We head to our usual café and get settled in, placing our order and taking off our jackets. When the waitress has gone, I turn to Lucy. "Well?"

"Well, what?" she asks, but I can see that she's trying not to smile.

"You've got a secret!" I insist, and she shrugs. Tim looks

bemused. "Spit it out!" I demand.

She takes a breath. "Miranda and I have decided ... well, we've decided that after the wedding, we're going to try for a baby," she finishes in a rush.

I gasp and clap my hands together, and The Supremes start 'oohing' the first notes of *Baby Love,* but Tim just looks confused. "How?" he asks innocently.

Lucy and I look at each other and try not to laugh. "How do you think?" I ask him, and the light dawns.

"A sperm bank?"

"That's right, genius," Lucy tells him.

"Cool!" he answers. Our food arrives and he takes a bite of his prawn-mayo baguette.

"I'm so pleased for you! How exciting!" I tell my best friend, hugging her, and she grins like an idiot. We start eating our own sandwiches and I ask who's going to be the one to carry the baby.

"Me," she answers proudly, and I squeal and half the diners in the café turn to stare, but I don't care. It's not every day that your best friend tells you that she's planning on becoming a mum. We chatter on about desirable donor characteristics (as close as possible to Miranda); names (absolutely *no* song titles – at which Tim looks bewildered); and which shops are the best for buying quality baby paraphernalia at reasonable prices (not many it turns out – they've already visited a few for research).

Tim munches away the whole time, letting the conversation wash over him, and I finally think to ask what's going on with Lola (*La-la-la-la-Lola!*). Apparently, it's going well.

"We went cycling on Saturday and I'm seeing her again on Wednesday," he tells us around a mouthful of crisps.

"And have you stuck to our advice?" Lucy asks suspiciously.

"Religiously."

"Good." Lucy and I shake hands and Tim rolls his eyes.

We finish eating and head back to the office. I manage to avoid Tom for the rest of the afternoon but others aren't so lucky. At five o'clock I scurry past his door with my head down, and make it to the lift without injury. Vanessa gazes back at him mournfully, but I ignore her plaintive wail.

The next morning, I arrive to find a small vase of flowers on my desk, with a note. I open the envelope and there's just one word written on it: *Sorry.* I look over at Tom's office but he's on the phone already, so I set to work with a smile on my face, a formerly grumpy Vanessa now perkily swinging her legs against my shoulder.

He's busy in meetings all morning, so I email him a quick *Thank you* just before lunch. I watch to see when he opens it and it's clear when he does because he looks out at me and grimaces then smiles. Vanessa giggles and I grin back like a fool, and that's when Jean calls to tell me that there's a delivery waiting for me at reception. I make my way over, confused when I spot a man standing there with a huge bunch of roses.

"Pippa Clayton?" he enquires, and I nod. He hands me the flowers and I murmur my thanks before he heads for the lift.

I shift the flowers to one arm so I can open the attached note, and blush when I see that they're from Max: *To a special lady*. Jean looks on curiously.

"Who're they from?" she asks, admiring the bouquet.

"Oh, er, a satisfied client," I tell her in embarrassment.

"Already? You must be doing well!" And I smile and make my way back to my desk. Tom does a double-take as I walk past his office and my blush deepens as I duck my head.

My workmates 'ooh' and 'aah' as they spot the beautiful blooms and Mike asks slyly if I've got a secret admirer. "Something like that," I mutter and thankfully no one pushes for more information.

I decide to eat lunch at my desk because I'm in the middle of a task that I don't want to interrupt, but most people head out. I'm so wrapped up in my work that I don't notice Tom approach until he clears his throat and I look up to spot him standing next to me.

He gestures to the roses. "Someone else who's been an arse?"

"Oh! No, just a gift," I reply awkwardly.

He frowns. "Is it your birthday?"

"No."

"Oh." He stands there with his head cocked expectantly, and after an awkward pause I give in and tell him they're from Max.

"Ah." He frowns, and I brace myself for a return of 'Grumpy Tom' but he just pats the desk and tells me that I must have impressed him. I release the breath I'd been holding and give a small smile, and he pats the desk again and tells me to make sure I take a break, then heads back to his office.

In the afternoon, Lucy catches my eye and points at the flowers then uses two fingers to point first at her eyes, then at mine. I roll my eyes and mouth 'later' and she's satisfied.

She's waiting at the lift for me at five o'clock, and we head for a coffee so I can catch her up on what's been happening.

"Why didn't you tell me you went out with Max?" she demands in a high-pitched voice when I've finished explaining.

"I thought it might be awkward. I didn't want people thinking I got a place on the creative team by sleeping with the client," I tell her in a hushed voice.

"I'd never think that!" she tells me, outraged, and I gesture for her to quieten down.

"I know, I'm sorry. I just felt a bit uncomfortable about the whole thing."

"Does Tom know?"

"Yes, he's the only one."

"What did you talk about?"

"Mostly ideas for a future campaign based on one of my designs. It was more of a business meeting than a date."

"And yet he's sent you roses and you're going to his house to do his portrait," Lucy says sceptically, and I blush and cringe.

She chuckles. "Well, he's certainly a catch – if you're into that type."

"Well, he's far too good looking for me," I answer, and she opens her mouth in denial but I hold up my hand. "Anyway, I'm sure he's just interested in what I've got to offer creatively."

"Yeah, right."

"It's true!" I insist to myself as much as to her. "He talent spotted me and now he's taken me under his wing – he probably sees me as an amusing project." But Lucy snorts.

"And what's with Tom anyway? Going around snapping everyone's head off and then choosing *you* to apologise to with flowers?"

I tell her about the exchange in Tom's office the previous day. Her eyebrows shoot up.

"He suggested you were unprofessional?"

"Well, no – he told me to *keep* it professional, but his tone of voice was quite peeved."

"Humph! What were you supposed to do – refuse a huge potential client? *He* schmoozes clients all the time – it's part of the job."

"He kissed me."

"Who, Tom?"

"No! Max."

"What, a snog?"

"No – more of a lingering peck on the lips."

"Hmm … maybe don't tell Tom that bit."

"I won't, don't worry."

"Do you like him?"

"Who, Tom?"

"No! Max."

"How could anyone not?"

She raises an eyebrow.

"Anyone *straight*," I correct.

"Are you … ready though? For a relationship, I mean. I know we joke around a lot, but – are you?"

I hesitate. "I don't know."

"It's been over two years," she reminds me gently.

I sigh. "I know."

She decides not to push it, and I'm grateful. We finish our coffees and hug goodbye on the street, then head our separate ways.

Chapter Eleven

The rest of the week and the next one pass uneventfully. Tom seems to go out of his way to act professionally around me and the atmosphere around the office is back to normal. Tim goes on a couple more dates with *La-la-la-la-Lola!* – he's even joined her book club – and Lucy and Miranda book their wedding at a hotel in the countryside and start researching sperm banks. Vanessa is hardly around, and my mind is unusually quiet.

Max calls me from his plane on Friday afternoon. "Are we still on for lunch tomorrow?" he asks after the formalities are over with.

"Er – we can leave it for another week if you need to rest after your trip?" I tell him uncertainly.

"No need," he dismisses. He rattles off an address in a *very* nice part of London and reminds me to bring my art materials before saying goodbye and I realise too late that I didn't thank him for the roses.

I deliberately dress casually on Saturday and arrive at his Georgian-style house wind-swept and rosy-cheeked. An older woman answers the door and I think at first that it's his mum before I realise that she must be some sort of housekeeper. She leads me through to a formal sitting room where Max is on the phone, but he finishes the call when he sees me and greets me with a kiss on each cheek.

"Did you walk all the way?" he asks in consternation, looking at my hiking books.

"Some of it," I answer breezily. I shrug off my jacket and the housekeeper takes it from me and asks Max what time he'd like lunch. He turns to me.

"Would you like lunch now or do you want to get started and we'll break for lunch in a bit?"

"Let's get started now," I answer.

He shows me around the ground floor of the house and I decide to do the portrait in the conservatory, where the light is the best. He watches in fascination as I unpack my materials and asks a few questions about the process. The housekeeper returns with refreshments and we're soon settled into our positions.

I start by outlining the shape of his head and the positions of his eyes, nose and mouth, my tongue sticking out to the side and a frown line between my eyebrows. It's soon obvious that he isn't used to sitting still by the way he fidgets and I have to admonish him more than once. He chuckles every time I do and I can tell that it's a novelty for him to let someone else be in charge for once. Eventually, I get my phone out and start playing a podcast that I like to listen to, and he settles down. We laugh at some of the comments on the show and I start to grow more relaxed in his company (and I haven't even had wine, reader!).

I move on to sketching in the finer details. As I look up to study his features in more depth, he flicks his eyes over my face as if studying me while I study him. At one point, I realise that I'm gazing at him quite intensely and haven't looked away, so I break the tension with a quick wink and he laughs.

We break for lunch at two – a delicious selection of sandwiches and pastries – and he admires the work that I've done so far, then we carry on for the rest of the afternoon. I try to capture the intense expression in his eyes, and the little uplift of his lips, the strength of his nose, the angle of his jaw and cheekbones. He sits still, gazing back at me, and I wonder what he's thinking. We haven't spoken for a while and I decide to ask him.

"I'm thinking about you," he tells me bluntly.

"What about me?"

"How you've managed to get under my skin in such a short amount of time, so that a day doesn't go by without me thinking of you and wondering what you're doing." And I actually gape at him.

He stands up and moves forward to crouch down before me, taking my materials out of my hands and putting them carefully to one side. Then he kisses me. And it's not a peck this time – even a lingering one – this is a full-blown, panties-bursting-into-flames snog of such intensity that I almost have an out-of-body experience.

Aretha Franklin bursts into *Natural Woman* and Vanessa 'Yippees!' as Max threads his fingers through the hair at the nape of my neck and moves his lips passionately against mine. I kiss him back with abandon, my toes curling, and just before I think I'm going to spontaneously combust, he eases back, caressing his lips against mine once, twice, three times before stopping. He stares into my eyes and I look back at him, dazed. His cheeks are flushed and his eyes are glittering. He looks at the door that leads into the house and seems about to say something but stops himself. "We'll take it slowly," he tells me in a low voice, and I nod. He kisses me again softly, and then he picks my materials up and puts them back in my hands before settling himself back on his seat.

My hands are shaking and I take a deep breath to steady myself. He chuckles, and I throw my pencil at him. We both laugh, and the tension eases. I work for a bit longer, then announce that I'm finished. He examines the portrait and declares it 'perfect', and I tell him he's biased.

"I'm notoriously hard to please," he defends himself with an arched eyebrow, and I roll my eyes. He kisses me again, walking me backwards until my back's against the wall, and we smooch until we're interrupted by the housekeeper clearing her throat. I blush, but she smiles at me kindly and asks Max if his 'guest' will be staying for dinner. He looks at me enquiringly but I'm meeting some uni friends so I have to decline.

He's disappointed, but to be honest I'm relieved to have an excuse; as much as I'm flattered and returned his kisses embarrassingly eagerly, it's all been a little sudden and intense. I need a bit of space. I do accept a lift back, though, and he drives me himself in his Merc.

We chat about the progress of the ad while he steers skilfully through the traffic. He's coming into the office on Wednesday and I tell him we'll have the changes he wanted finalised by then; I can tell that he's pleased. I wonder what he's like when he's not and ask him.

"I always get what I want in the end, one way or another," he tells me.

"Like a Mafia boss?" I ask archly.

"Not quite," he answers wryly.

"How then?"

"I surround myself with talented people and only accept perfection."

"But no one can be perfect all the time."

"True, but too many slip-ups and they find themselves getting replaced. That's business."

"What about in your personal life?"

"What do you mean?"

"Do you expect girlfriends to be perfect, too, or *they* get replaced?"

He squirms. "It depends what you mean by 'perfect'."

I laugh. "I think you just answered my question." He grimaces. "I warn you now," I say as the car pulls up outside my building, "I'm far from being the perfect woman."

He leans over to kiss me. "You're perfectly adorable." I smile and hop out of the car. He waits for me to go inside before he drives away, and I head up the stairs to get ready for my night out while Katrina and the Waves belt out *Walking on Sunshine.*

I meet Jemima and Gideon at a bar that we used to frequent as students, which has become our traditional meeting place. We all studied art together and they started dating in our second year. Gideon is a graphic designer and Jemima is on maternity leave after having their second child. She spends a large chunk of the first hour venting about the amount of weight that she's gained and how the kids are both still waking up several times per night. I tut sympathetically and give her a hug when she starts crying messily. Gideon stands there looking overwhelmed and awkward – he's never been good with displays of emotion – so I send him to get another round of drinks and lead Jemima over to a booth that's just become vacant.

"Tell me all about it," I say gently, and she bursts into an outpouring of frustrated motherhood.

Gideon returns with the drinks and quickly decides that he needs the toilet and scurries away.

"I'm just so fed up of having shit under my fingernails and boobs that leak like hosepipes," she finishes on a wail and I grimace at the image but continue to rub her shoulder reassuringly.

"This stage won't last forever," I tell her.

"It feels like it will." She hiccups and makes a grab for her wine glass. "I shouldn't be drinking while I'm breastfeeding, but sod it!" she declares rebelliously, taking a massive gulp. I look around for Gideon but he's nowhere to be seen.

"Are you getting much support from family?" I ask desperately as The Beatles start blasting *Help!*

She snorts. "My mum's useless, as you know, and Gideon's

mum is just a patronising arse, quite frankly." She wipes her nose with the back of her hand and I hurry to retrieve a tissue from my bag for her. She blows noisily and hands it back to me. "I just feel like everything I do is wrong!" she wails again, and the tears start flowing once more.

"I'm sure it's normal to feel like this," I tell her. "You're being too hard on yourself – you're doing a *great* job!" It's true – I'd visited them at their house a few weeks before Christmas, and, yes, the house was a tip and Jemima was still in her dressing gown at one in the afternoon, but there was no doubt that the children are well-loved and well-looked after. I offer to babysit for her whenever she wants – sometimes people just need a break – and she gives me a watery smile in appreciation.

Gideon returns looking wary, and Jemima decides to visit the loo to re-touch her makeup. I tentatively broach the subject of post-natal depression with him and wonder if a trip to the GP would help; he nods in relief and says that he'll talk to her about it when she's calmer.

When Jemima returns, we head to the restaurant. I link arms with her as we walk and she smiles and squeezes me. "I'm sorry for off-loading on you."

"Don't be silly – that's what friends are for."

"I do love my kids, but it's hard work being a mum," she tells me, then she looks at me in horror, her eyes wide and her hand over her mouth. "Oh my God!" she says, looking appalled. "I'm so sorry, I didn't think –"

I rush to reassure her, but her cheeks glow in embarrassment for the rest of the way.

I steer the conversation in a new direction once we've ordered our food, telling them about my new role at work and how much fun it is being creative and getting paid for it. Gideon agrees, and tells us about some of the projects that he's been working on lately. Jemima joins in with some funny stories from when she was working – she's an illustrator – and I can tell that it's doing her the world of good to be out of the house and engaging in adult conversation. She switched to water once we arrived, and there have been no more tears.

They have to be home by ten for Gideon's mum, who's babysitting the kids ("I'll get back to find the children's drawers re-arranged and that my skirting boards have been inspected for dust," Jemima murmurs to me as we shrug into our coats, and I grimace sympathetically). They see me into a taxi and we wave goodbye until I'm out of sight. On the radio Tammy Wynette starts complaining about how hard it is to be a woman, and the driver switches to another station.

Max texts me on Sunday.

How was your night out?

Good, thanks, except my friend seems to be suffering from the baby blues ☹ *What did you get up to?*

Working, mostly. Sorry to hear that about your friend x

All work and no play … ;-) Thanks – I think she'll be OK x

My playmate abandoned me just when things were beginning to get interesting! ;-)

I'm glad you enjoyed the podcast so much – it's one of my favs ;-)

Ha! What are you doing on Valentine's evening???

Nothing?

Come out with me? x

Okay x

☺

☺

See you on Wednesday x

See you then, boss!

Cheeky

Chapter Twelve

On Monday, Lucy grabs me as soon as I arrive at work and bundles me into the ladies'.

"What are you *doing*?" I squeal.

"Give me all the gossip about Saturday," she demands, smirking at my discomposure.

"Saturday? Hmm … I can't quite remember what I did on Saturday," I tease and she slaps me lightly on the arm.

"Don't keep me in suspense!"

"Okay, okay! Well … I sketched Max's portrait in his conservatory … we had lunch … I sketched some more … he told me he couldn't stop thinking about me –" She squeals at this. "– and then he kissed me."

She grabs me. "Another peck?"

"Nope. A proper, stomach-flipping, panty-melting smooch against the wall."

Her jaw drops, then a huge shit-eating grin spreads across her face. "And then what?"

"And then – nothing. We agreed to take it slowly. He invited me to dinner, but I was meeting up with Jemima and

Gideon." She sags in disappointment and I decide to take pity on her. "He did text me yesterday to ask if I was free on Valentine's Day though."

"I hope you said yes."

I nod, and she squeals again and claps her hands. Lisa walks in at that moment and gives us a funny look, but we ignore her and she goes into a cubicle. We head to our desks and get started on the day's tasks.

I spend the morning with Simon fine-tuning our storyboards for Max's visit on Wednesday. We're pleased with the changes that we've made based on his feedback and feel pretty confident about presenting them to him. We're just finishing up liaising with other members of the team when Tom calls me into his office. Of course, Vanessa wakes up and starts fussing with her hair in readiness as we make our way over to him. "Hussy," I mutter at her as I walk past Lisa's desk, but fortunately she's on the phone and doesn't hear.

Tom shuts the door behind me and gestures for me to sit down. He asks how the storyboards are going and I tell him they're just about ready, and he nods then shifts uncomfortably in his chair.

"You want to know how Saturday went," I say into the pause.

He blinks. "Well, I wasn't going to just blurt it out like that, but …"

"But that's the real reason why you called me in here."

He squirms, then nods.

I sigh. "I'm seeing him again on Valentine's Day."

"Oh." He frowns, and I can't quite make out the expression that's in his eyes.

"Is there a policy against employees dating clients or something?"

"Well, no, but … it's unusual and …"

It's my turn to frown. "And what?"

"Well, are you sure he's … right for you?"

My eyebrows shoot up. "I'm not sure that's any of your business."

He opens his mouth then closes it again. We stare at each other. Finally, he presses his hands down on his desk and says softly, "Well, I just hope that he deserves you."

I relent. "Why wouldn't he?"

He hesitates. "He has a … reputation."

"What sort of a reputation?"

"Of going through women like most men go through underwear," he answers bluntly.

"Well, it's just a date – it's not like I'm going to *marry* him or anything," I say crossly.

He raises his hands. "Okay, fine. I'm only saying this because I … care … about you. I don't want to see you get hurt."

I nod stiffly. He opens his mouth as if to say something else but then clamps his lips closed.

"How's Melanie?" I ask, a little pointedly. He grimaces, and Vanessa growls at me. There's another silence. "Truce?" I finally ask softly, and he jerks his head and reaches out his hand. We shake.

I stand on trembling legs and head to the door. I pause with my hand on the handle. "I appreciate the warning," I tell him without turning around, then I walk out the door.

I spend the afternoon helping out on another ad and brooding over the conversation. So Max dates a lot of women – he's an attractive, successful man, why wouldn't he? Doesn't mean he's a cad. He's admitted himself that he expects perfection out of the people he surrounds himself with, and with impossibly high standards like that he's probably disappointed a *lot*. I decide I'll take things a step at a time, and not let my – fragile as it is - heart run away with me. Vanessa huffs at this, and I flick her away. Satisfied, I throw myself into my designs for a condom commercial, bopping away to Olivia Newton-John as she sings *Physical* at full volume.

Max arrives for the pitch on Wednesday looking completely delicious. Tom greets him at reception and the two of them together look like an ad for a corporate dating website. I must admit, I would swipe right for both of them. Vanessa purrs in agreement and I'm surprised when The Weather Girls don't burst into a rendition of *It's Raining Men*.

I wave and carry on helping Simon to set up the last few things for the meeting. Max winks back with that sexy smirk. Tom pretends he hasn't seen it.

Soon the team is settled around the table in the conference room and there's a brief bustle as coffees are poured and notepads arranged. So far this time, I've managed to maintain my dignity – I'm pleased to say that I haven't displayed my knickers once, reader, and we're already five minutes into the meeting.

Tom welcomes Max and summarises the progress that's been made since his last visit before handing over to Simon, who talks him through the storyboards. Max looks over the presentation thoughtfully, rubbing his finger over his full bottom lip, and finally gives his approval. He asks a couple of questions about the next stage of production and other members of the team are called on to contribute. I'm fascinated by the process and listen attentively, taking copious notes.

I get a little carried away doodling a stylised flow-chart, and when I look up, it's to find that everyone is staring at me. I blink and wonder what I've missed. I was doing so well, damn it!

"Max was asking if he could see what progress you've made on the series that you came up with to advertise the Wild Spirit brand as a whole, Pippa," Tom tells me, trying to hide an amused smile. "I told him that you've already been working on it in preparation for possible production in the future."

"Oh!" I look at Max, who isn't bothering to hide his own amusement. I feel my cheeks turn red. "Of course! Shall I fetch the revised storyboards?"

"No need," Max says before Tom can respond. "I'll stop by your desk after we've finished here."

The meeting draws to a close soon after and I linger behind the others to escort Max to my desk. When just the three of us are left, I get a sense of déjà vu and wonder what's in store for me this time. I gape as Max turns to Tom and says bluntly, "I hope it's not a problem that I'm dating Pippa." To give Tom credit, he doesn't bat an eyelid.

"Not at all," he says in a smooth voice, and I nearly snort.

"Good." Max turns to me. "Shall we?" I nod, and he puts his hand on my lower back as I lead the way out of the room. Tom watches with hooded eyes.

"Why did you say that?" I demand in mild exasperation once we're out of ear shot.

"Just wanted to lay my cards on the table – to make sure that you'd encounter no difficulties by dating a client. I find that straight-talking achieves the best results."

"You've done this before then?" I ask archly.

"You know what I mean, madam."

We arrive at my desk and he leans against it as I show him my work for stage one of the campaign. We discuss stage two, where more of the colours are picked out and the relationship between the characters develops further, and he asks for more detail on voice-overs and supers – the text that's placed over the visuals. We talk for more than half an hour before he looks at his watch and says regretfully that he's got another meeting to go to. I walk him to the lift, and when Jean's not looking, he sneaks a quick peck on the cheek. Vanessa giggles and I purse my lips at his brazenness but can't stop a small smile from emerging. He steps jauntily into the lift and I roll my eyes when he salutes as the doors slide shut.

I meet up with Tim for lunch. He's down in the dumps because Lola has told him that she thinks they ought to see other people, and I tell him gently that it obviously wasn't meant to be.

"I just don't get it," he says. "I did everything right this time. I was attentive, but not claustrophobic – and there was a *real* spark between us – not like when I was with Gloria."

"Sometimes you can do everything right, and it still isn't enough," I say softly.

"Maybe I should just give up on women for a while," he answers, looking glum.

"Or maybe just stop trying so hard," I suggest softly, "and it will happen when it's supposed to happen."

He looks surprised at the novelty of this idea but bites his lip and starts nodding.

I steer the conversation to work, and he talks enthusiastically about a new account that he's been put in charge of. We finish our lunch and head back to the office where we stop for a quick chat with Lucy, who ate at her desk because she's got a tight deadline to meet. Before I return to my desk, we arrange a date for dress shopping for the wedding.

The next morning when I wake up, I'm aching all over and can't stop shivering. I feel exhausted. I call in sick and tell Jean I've got the flu and she tells me she'll pass the message on to Tom and reminds me to drink plenty of fluids. I take some paracetamol and get a fresh glass of water and go back to bed.

Lucy texts me at lunchtime asking if I need anything but I don't want to put her out so I tell her I just need to rest. It's pretty crap living on your own when you're ill. I stick a podcast on so I don't feel so miserable and alone. I fall back to sleep half way through the afternoon and I only wake up when the doorbell goes at quarter past six in the evening.

I haul myself out of bed, expecting to hear Lucy's voice through the intercom, but instead it's Tom's. I buzz him through, too sick to be too surprised or even care much about my appearance. I'm in my teddy bear pyjamas and dressing gown and I suspect my hair is sticking out wildly, but all I can think about is trying not to faint. I leave the door to the flat open for him and fall onto the couch.

Within a minute, I hear a knock and he enters the cosy living room. He's ruddy cheeked from the cold outside and he looks gorgeous in his long overcoat and scarf, like a catalogue model. I take this all in as if I'm in a dream while he looks around the room and finally spots me on the sofa.

"Pippa, hi – thought I'd come and check on you on my way home from work, er, since I live nearby and all," he says with a half-concerned, half-what-the-hell-am-I-doing-here look as he sits and perches on the edge of the armchair.

"That's very kind of you," I croak, and he frowns and looks at me more closely.

"Gosh, you *are* ill, aren't you?" And I burst into tears. Startled, he jumps up and reaches out to me, but hesitates as if unsure of what to do, then he shakes himself and comes and sits next to me, enclosing me in his arms. I lean against him, uncaring that I haven't showered today and probably smell pretty bad. It's just nice to be held.

He rubs my back and we sit there like that for some time.

My crying gradually subsides and I take a few shuddering breaths. Eventually, I murmur 'Thanks' and try to move away, but he holds me tighter and I settle back against him, sighing.

"Have you had anything to eat today?" he finally murmurs and I shake my head.

"I haven't really felt like eating."

"Well, you should try to eat something – even if it's just toast." He eases back and stands up, taking off his coat and laying it over the armchair before heading to the kitchen. I lie down and hear him rummaging in the breadbin and then the sound of the toaster being pressed down. The tap goes on and he comes back through with a glass of water for me. He puts it on the coffee table and sits back down, his sleeves rolled up and his tie loosened.

"Nice place you've got here," he tells me awkwardly, and I give him a small smile. "I like your fridge magnets," he adds, and this takes me so much by surprise that I manage a tired laugh.

"No one's ever complimented me on my fridge magnets before," I tell him.

"I like to be different."

"You're certainly that."

"Which one's your favourite?" he asks curiously.

I think for a minute. The selection is all miniature versions of famous works of art – Picasso's *Guernica,* Van Gogh's *Sunflowers,* Da Vinci's *Mona Lisa,* Edvard Munch's *The Scream,* Dali's *The Persistence of Memory* etcetera. "Probably *The Starry Night,*" I decide at last.

"Why that one?"

"It has a dream-like quality about it that I like."

"Mmm. I think I'd pick that one too."

The toast pops, and he gets up and heads back into the kitchen. I'm completely bemused by his presence in my flat, but I've got to admit it's nice to have someone looking after me.

He returns with a plate, and I sit up and nibble at the offering while he looks on in approval. I manage to eat half of the toast and then tell him that I need some more paracetamol. I start to get up but he jumps up and tells me that he'll get it. I explain which cupboard it's in and he finds the packet quickly and brings it to me. I swallow a couple with water and lie back down.

"You should be in bed," he tells me with a frown.

"I was."

"Oh, shit! Sorry," he grimaces.

"It's okay," I tell him, but getting up like this has exhausted me and I'm starting to flag.

"No – I'll head off and let you get some rest."

I smile gratefully and start to get up, but I wobble and nearly fall over and he catches me before any damage is done. He scoops me up into his arms and asks me where the bedroom is, and I point and tell him and he carries me through effortlessly. I feel like a bride on her wedding night as he crosses the threshold and eases me down onto my bed, but the effect is ruined as he pulls the covers over me.

He leaves for a minute then returns with my fresh water, picking up the stale glass that was on my bedside table. With his free hand, he smooths back the hair from my forehead and I almost expect him to kiss me as he hesitates, but if he was going to, he obviously changes his mind because he murmurs for me to get some rest and then he leaves, closing the door softly behind him. I hear the tap running again as he rinses out my glass, then the door of the flat opens and shuts, and he's gone.

I fall asleep wondering about the look in his eyes as he'd gazed down at me, stroking my hair.

Chapter Thirteen

I'm still ill the next day so I call in sick again. I get texts from Lucy, Tim, Simon and Evie throughout the morning, and then Max texts in the late afternoon. He's in New York, and he tells me he's looking forward to our Valentine's date, which is the week after next. I don't bother telling him I'm ill; I just say *Me too x* and ask what we're doing.

It's a surprise ;-) he answers, and I smile and snuggle down into my covers.

Tom surprises me by turning up after work again, and he sheepishly tells me that he promised Lucy that he'd look in on me. I'm feeling a bit better by now, and up to eating something more substantial, so he makes me an omelette and pours me some orange juice which he'd picked up on the way. I sit at the kitchen table while he cooks and watch him working, occasionally pointing out where he can find the utensils he needs and puzzling over his presence in my flat once again.

"You know, I'm not sure homecare is in your job description," I finally tell him, a little frown line between my eyebrows.

"Kindness should be in the job description for being a human being," he answers without turning around, but I can tell that he's blushing from the small part of the side of his face that's visible.

"Well, thank you – I appreciate it."

"You're welcome." He places a plate in front of me and sits down opposite me to eat his own. We eat in companionable silence.

"How's Melanie?" I ask eventually.

He finishes chewing a mouthful and I can tell that he's thinking of how to answer. "She's well," he says at last, but I can tell there's more he's not saying.

"But?"

He grimaces. "You can read me like a book, can't you?" He sighs. "Things have been a bit ... tense ... lately, that's all."

"I'm sorry to hear that. I hope you can work through it. I like Melanie a lot."

"Yeah, she's great." However, I sense another 'but'.

"How long have you been together?" I ask curiously.

"Since we were at college."

My eyebrows shoot up. "Wow. That's a *long* time."

"I know," he sighs, and I'm tempted to ask why they haven't married or started a family yet, but realise that that would be the height of nosiness. "I've started to feel like we're still together out of habit," he adds quietly.

"It's normal to feel like that when you're in a long-term

relationship," I tell him sympathetically.

He hesitates, then asks how long my husband and I were together for. "Eight years," I answer, then get up to pour myself another orange juice so I won't have to say any more about it. Fortunately, he takes the hint. We finish our omelettes and he clears away the dishes. Before he leaves, he asks me if I'll be alright over the weekend and I tell him I'm feeling a lot better.

"Hopefully see you Monday then," he says, shrugging into his coat, and I nod. He looks down at me lingeringly as I stand by the open door, and I realise that I can't read him as well as he thinks because I have no idea what's going on in his head. Then he's gone, and I head back to bed where I receive another text from Lucy checking up on me. I confirm that Tom's been and that I've eaten and she's satisfied, but insists on visiting me tomorrow to see for herself that I'm okay.

She comes with Miranda at lunchtime. I've managed to have a shower and get dressed, so I'm presentable when they arrive, not that they'd care if I was still in my PJs; I once turned up to their place and Lucy opened the door to me stark naked.

They've brought bagels and we sit eating them and looking through bridal catalogues for most of the afternoon before they have to head off to visit Miranda's parents. I spend the rest of the day resting and reading some more of *Jane Eyre* and lusting over Mr. Rochester.

On Sunday, I'm almost back to normal, and I decide that

I'll be okay for work tomorrow. I call my parents and Mum tells me off when I reveal that I've been sick and didn't tell them.

"I'd have come down to look after you!" she scolds.

"That's why I didn't tell you," I say drily, and she tuts. "I was fine," I add. "I just needed to rest – and besides, some work colleagues looked in on me," and this satisfies her.

I'm welcomed back to work warmly by my colleagues on Monday and I throw myself into my tasks. Tom stops by to check if I'm really well enough to be back and I assure him that I am and thank him again for checking in on me. He mutters something incomprehensible and then walks away. *Men!* I think, and Vanessa giggles. She was notably absent during my illness, but popped up again on Sunday. She pouted when I accused her of being a 'fair-weather friend' and has given me the cold shoulder ever since, which has bothered me not one jot.

I spend the next two weeks firmly focussed on my work. I'm working on a few different accounts now and still 'apprenticing' in each department when I get chance. Max calls me a couple of times from America and we exchange a few flirty texts which make me blush and set my heart racing every time. I go to lunch with Tim and Lucy a few times and we mostly discuss weddings and babies, and Tom is back to being 'Mr. Professional', though sometimes I sense his eyes on me. However, when I look in his direction, he's always busy, so it must be my imagination.

Valentine's Day falls on a Tuesday, and I get a text from Max in the morning telling me he'll pick me up at seven and that I should wear casual clothes. Intrigued, I send a quick text back then finish getting ready for work. I've organised a 'Wear Pink for Breast Cancer' day, so I dress in a pair of pink tights and a love-heart patterned blouse before rushing to the bus stop.

When I arrive, I pop on my pink bunny ears headband and make sure that Jean has the tub for donations ready on reception. I put in my own and then head the rest of the way into the office, pleased to see that pretty much everyone has joined in. Evie has a pale pink dress on; Mike, Stan and Simon are wearing pink ties in various shades; and Llewellyn actually has pink *trousers* on. Tim arrives wearing another pink tie and Lucy rocks a pair of hot pink high heels when she steps out of the lift. The rest of the staff have also joined in, some wearing pink flowers in their lapels or hair. Even Lisa has participated, wearing a pink skirt that actually looks rather good on her. I tell her so and she smiles with pleasure, and I decide to let bygones be bygones. Life's too short to hold a grudge.

Tom steps out of the lift wearing a pink shirt, and *damn* if it doesn't look amazing on him. Everything seems to slow down as Patti LaBelle starts gushing *Voulez vous coucher avec moi* and he strides past reception. Vanessa mews in my ear and I catch myself staring. He tweaks one of my bunny ears when he passes me, and I smile stupidly before remembering I've got work to do (and that *he's* got a girlfriend). *Damn!* A girl can look, can't she?

At lunchtime, I check how the donations are doing and we're at just over a hundred pounds. Then I catch up with

Tim and Lucy at our favourite café. I get a few funny looks before I realise that I still have my bunny ears on but quickly decide that I don't care. Lucy and I commiserate with Tim over his first ever time being single on Valentine's Day and I finally reveal to him that I have a date with Max Wild. In typical Tim style, his only response is 'Cool!' and then he continues munching on his chicken tikka baguette.

"Where's he taking you?" Lucy asks curiously, and I tell her I don't know. "Maybe he'll whisk you off in his private jet to see the opera, like Richard Gere did for Julia Roberts – only in Paris."

"He said to dress casually."

"Hmm, can't be the opera then. Guess you'll find out later."

"What're you and Miranda doing tonight?"

"Watching a film then going for a curry."

"Yummy!"

We finish our lunch and head back to the office where I discover a heart balloon bouquet and teddy bear waiting for me on my desk with a note saying *Happy Valentine's Day – see you tonight. Max x*

"Your admirer again?" asks Mike, and I smile and blush. I see Tom looking over but he doesn't mention it when I'm called into his office to discuss a project later in the afternoon.

After work, I check the final total for the donations - £176 – and remember to remove my bunny ears before I leave the building. The bus is a little late so I don't get home til after six. I dive into the shower then rush to get dressed for my date with Max while The Pointer Sisters sing *I'm So Excited* and Vanessa bounces on my shoulder. I go with the 'figure-hugging jeans and low-cut top' look then spend the rest of the time debating which shoes to wear.

The buzzer goes and I bark, "Shoes?" into the intercom. A masculine chuckle responds and then, "It doesn't matter – you're going to be changing them. Just make sure you've got some socks."

Completely bemused, I buzz him through then slip on a pair of high-heeled shoes and stuff a pair of socks into my bag just as he arrives at the door to my flat. He pecks me on the cheek, murmuring, "You look ravishing," then looks around curiously. Thank God I did a quick tidy up last night. I offer him a tour but apparently we have a half-seven booking so I lock up and follow him out to the car. He's driving again, and I settle in to the familiar seat as he pulls out into traffic.

"So, are you going to tell me where we're going?" I ask tartly.

"You'll see when we get there. All I'll say is that I thought we'd do something a little less formal than the last time we went out – have a little fun."

I arch my eyebrow. "Max Wild – are you *letting your hair down?*" I tease.

He clucks his tongue. "I do sometimes, you know."

"Bet you'll still limit yourself to one glass of wine."

"I'm not sure they serve wine where we're going."

"Well, there'd better be gin," I grumble, and he laughs.

Twenty minutes later, we pull up in front of a bowling complex.

"Ahhh!" I say as the penny drops.

"I hope you're not disappointed."

"No way – bowling's great fun."

"Even though it's something active?"

"Just watch out for your toes," I warn him, and he grins, but I'm half-serious.

We check in and, of course, Max has booked a VIP lane for the entire evening, complete with table service and complimentary champagne. We're just changing our shoes when Tom and Melanie walk in. We all do a comedy double-take and then greet each other like long-lost friends.

"Great minds think alike," Tom murmurs to me with a smirk.

"They *do*," I respond, giving him a sideways look as I remember those words exchanged in the Chinese take-away.

"Do you think they do twenty-seven and fifty-three here?" he asks innocently, and I snort. Max and Melanie look at us in bemusement, and I wave it away, claiming it to be a work joke.

To my surprise, Max asks them if they'd like to join us in our lane and play two against two, but I see the competitive gleam in his eye as he sizes up Tom and I soon get the picture. Tom seems excited by the idea too, and Melanie doesn't seem to mind, so Max squares it with the girl on the desk and we head over to the VIP lane once they've changed their shoes.

"I've got a feeling this is going to turn into a *who's got the biggest dick* competition," I murmur out of the side of my mouth to Melanie, and she giggles.

"I heard that," Tom calls back.

"So did I, madam," Max tells me in an admonishing tone, and I stick my tongue out at him and he grins.

While they program our names into the computer, a waitress brings over our champagne and Melanie and I start on it straight away. We order a selection of nibbles and the waitress heads off.

Tom bowls first and gets a strike straight away, and the competition is ON.

Chapter Fourteen

I'm not bad at bowling and Max high-fives me when I get a respectable spare when it's my turn. Like Tom, Max gets a strike, but Melanie's first ball ends up in the left gutter. Tom calls out supportively when she bowls her second ball, and she manages to knock down five.

The second round starts and Tom gets another strike while Max gets a spare; I knock down eight pins and Melanie gets six. Survivor starts singing *Eye of the Tiger* over the sound-system and the competitive gleam brightens in the men's eyes. I roll mine at Melanie and she smiles sweetly. We play another two rounds and then the nibbles arrive.

Tom and I dive for the nachos at the same time and everyone laughs. While we're eating, Max puts his arm around my waist and Tom follows the action with his eyes. I've noticed that apart from coaching her through each bowl, Tom and Melanie haven't really talked to each other much, and they certainly haven't touched. In fact, they both seem a bit miserable to be forced to sit together. I make a point of including Melanie in the conversation when work talk dominates a bit too much, and Max winks at me.

We finish off the game and Max and I win by eight points. We all shake hands and Tom demands a re-match. We decide to have a toilet break first, and Tom and Melanie head off in separate directions to use the loos.

"Trouble in paradise?" Max asks when they've gone.

"I think so," I grimace.

He shakes his head and reaches for his glass, then obviously decides to change the subject.

"I've got to say," he begins, "you've impressed me tonight."

"Why?" I ask archly. "Didn't you think I had it in me?"

"It's not your bowling skill that I'm talking about – it's the fact that you haven't fallen over yet."

I slap him lightly on the arm and he chuckles. I tell him about the year I tripped over the mike stand and fell off the stage at the Christmas party and he laughs his head off then pulls me in for a kiss. We're still smooching when Tom arrives back and clears his throat awkwardly. I blush and tidy my hair, then Melanie returns and we order some more drinks, then I decide that I need to use the toilet as well.

When I get back, Max is asking Melanie about teaching, and Tom is working on polishing off the nachos. I sidle up beside him and sneak my hand out and grab the last few and he swats me hard on the butt. I freeze and he turns red.

I look over to where Max and Melanie are talking but they're oblivious. I feel heat flood my body (*that* kind of heat) and I risk a look up at Tom through my eyelashes to discover his eyes glittering down into mine. He inhales sharply and mutters something that sounds like '*Fuck!*' before turning on his heel and grabbing a bowling ball. Vanessa is panting in my ear and I take a huge swig of my champagne in an attempt to cool myself down. Tom's ball ends up in the gutter and he comes back for another, tight-lipped and avoiding eye-contact. This time, he gets all of the pins down, and I swap places with him without saying a word, but I can feel that my cheeks are still flushed (no, not *those* cheeks, naughty!).

Unsurprisingly, I only get one pin down with my first ball and then only three more with my second. I swap places with Melanie and put my hand in Max's. He raises it to his lips and kisses it and I smile at him. I glance over at Tom and see him working hard to watch Melanie's performance, but something in the tension of his body tells me he's aware of everything I do.

For the rest of the game, I stay by Max when he's not bowling, and when he is I talk to Melanie or sit on my own, drinking my champagne and gradually getting more and more tipsy. My performance in this game sucks, and Tom and Melanie end up winning by over twenty points, though neither team did as well as they did in the first game.

Tom says they have to head off then – they have a table booked in a nearby restaurant. He shakes hands with Max and nods in my direction. Relieved, I hug Melanie goodbye and wish them a happy Valentine's Day.

Max pulls me down to sit next to him when they're gone and nuzzles my neck. It feels delicious, and Vanessa sighs. When he pulls back and looks at me, there's heat in his eyes and I feel an answering warmth in my belly. He kisses me on the lips and only stops when the waitress arrives. We agree to have another game and order something more substantial to eat.

"You didn't mind me inviting them to join us, did you?" he asks when she's gone.

"Of course not," I say brightly, and try to put what happened with Tom out of my mind.

He decides to bowl with his left hand to give me a fighting chance, and I roll my eyes at the twinkle in his. Now that we're on our own, he decides that I need help with my technique, and he comes up behind me under the pretence of improving my stance. He bends me over and puts his hand over mine, guiding the direction of my swing but chuckling low in my ear the whole time. I decide to get my own back by wriggling my butt in his crotch and he inhales sharply. Of course, the ball ends up in the gutter, but I don't care as he turns me around and walks me backwards into the cocoon of our VIP seating area and starts kissing me with abandon.

Eventually, I break the kiss and breathlessly accuse him of trying to distract me so he can win. He laughs and lets me go. With my second ball I manage to knock down all the pins and the competitive light returns to his eyes. We play a few rounds, then take a break when our food arrives. I'm glad to have something to soak up the alcohol.

While we eat, I ask Max about his family back in Australia. He returned there for Christmas, which he spent at his parents' house. He tells me he has two brothers and a sister, and I express how wonderful that sounds to an only child like me. He grimaces and says, "You wouldn't think that if you'd witnessed some of the fights we've had over the years," but I can tell that he's fond of them.

We finish the game, which of course Max wins by a mile

despite playing left-handed, then we head to a bar for a drink. He switched to water after one glass of champagne at the bowling alley, and I decide it's a good idea to go for a non-alcoholic cocktail. He cocks an eyebrow when I place my order, and I sheepishly tell him that I'm feeling a little drunk. "I guess I'd better not take advantage of you then," he smirks and pulls me in for a light kiss.

We watch the couples dancing for a while before Max takes my glass and places it down on a table, then he's taking my hand and leading me out to join them. You won't be surprised to hear that I have two left feet, reader, but fortunately, being Valentine's Day, the DJ's playing a selection of slow songs which are ideal for rocking to-and-fro to and smooching. Currently, Phyllis Nelson's urging everyone to *Move Closer* and I don't need to be told twice.

At eleven thirty, the bar closes and we head back to Max's car hand-in-hand. Our breath fogs in the frigid air as we walk. He asks me if I've had a good time, and, contentedly, I tell him that I have.

The ride back to my flat is quiet and companionable. When he's not shifting gears, he puts his hand over mine and strokes his thumb lightly over my finger. Finally, we arrive on my road. He parks the car and walks me to my door and I'm tempted to invite him inside. But then I remember Tom's warning and my promise to myself to take it slowly. Max looks down at me with hooded eyes and I think he senses my indecision because he leans in to kiss me softly on the lips, murmuring that he'll call me, then he takes the key out of my hand and unlocks the door and I walk through it, shutting it quietly behind me.

I get ready for bed, wondering where things with Max are

heading. I deliberately don't think about Tom.

I dread facing Tom the next day when I arrive at work so I hang around reception chatting to Jean until I see someone enter his office before I brave the walk past the glass front to get to my desk. Fortunately, he seems to have decided to avoid me too because even when he's free he doesn't send for me, and as the morning goes on, I gradually start to relax.

I catch up with Lucy at lunchtime and fill her in on my date with Max (minus the incident with Tom). She's disappointed that he didn't sweep me away somewhere romantic on his private jet but I reassure her that I had a great time anyway.

Max texts as I'm heading back to my desk.

How's your head today? ;-)

Fine thank you, boss x

Sigh. Are you free for dinner on Saturday night, madam?

Yes x

Pick you up at seven? x

OK, boss x

Grrr ;-)

The afternoon passes swiftly. Tom still doesn't summon me and before I know it, it's home time. However, I decide to pop to the ladies' before I head off and I walk back out rummaging in my bag for my bus pass only to bump right into his hard chest. He grabs my arms automatically and then drops his hands like he's been burned and steps back. We both turn bright red and mutter an apology, then stand there awkwardly, not knowing where to look.

"How was the rest of your evening?" he finally asks.

"Good, good! Er, how was yours?"

He grimaces.

"Oh," I say sympathetically. Perhaps they had an argument?

We stand there in silence for a few moments, then we both start speaking at once.

"Look, about last night –"

"I want to apologise for –"

We stop and laugh uncomfortably. "You go first," I tell him.

"I was just saying that I'd like to apologise for last night. I just reacted without thinking but it was completely out of line and –"

"It's fine."

He clears his throat and reaches into his pocket. "Anyway, I have something I want to give you by way of saying sorry. I've had it on my fridge for years but I saw it last night when I got home and thought it would be a good addition to your collection." And he pulls out a fridge magnet depicting Van Gogh's *Irises* and hands it to me.

"Thank you," I say, genuinely touched. He shifts uneasily and I can tell that he's embarrassed, so I tell him I'd better be going if I'm going to catch my bus and he nods and steps back to let me pass. It's only when I'm halfway home that it crosses my mind that bumping into him might not have been an accident.

The rest of the week goes smoothly. I don't have much to

do with Tom but when I do, he's totally professional. Max calls on Thursday night and we spend half the time talking about how the production of the ad's going and half of it flirting shamelessly. On Saturday morning, I go dress shopping with Lucy.

We're in our third bridal shop before she decides to go for a trouser suit over a dress, and we spend our time at the next three shops trying on their limited selections. My favourite has a fitted lace bodice with three-quarter length trousers and looks great with killer high heels, but Lucy's undecided between that and another that has full-length culotte-style trousers and lace sleeves. Vanessa's in her element and seems to love everything.

We break for lunch to take stock of things, and as she sits biting her nails, I remind her gently that she doesn't need to make a decision today. She pulls a face and barely eats a thing.

We decide to head back and try the two outfits on again. I take photos of her in each and she decides she needs to sleep on it, which I think is for the best. While we're there, we check out some bridesmaid dresses and get a feel for the sort of look we might go for, but we want Miranda to be involved so we agree to arrange another date when she's available.

"I thought today would be fun but I just feel stressed," she tells me over a coffee in a high street café once we've decided to call it a day. I pull a sympathetic face. "I just want everything to be perfect," she adds with a sigh.

"It will be. It doesn't matter what outfit you wear – you could turn up in a black bag and Miranda wouldn't care. The point is that you'll be there and she'll be there and you're promising to spend the rest of your lives together – the rest is just window-dressing."

"You're right."

"Either of those outfits will do. You look knock-out in both. Even *I* fancied you a bit when I saw you in them, so Miranda will definitely be blown away," I wink, and she grins.

"I guess I just thought we'd spend the day having a girly giggle breezing through the options and drinking champagne while Cyndi Lauper sings *Girls Just Want to Have Fun,* and that I'd eventually spot the perfect get-up and just *know* when I saw it."

"I think that only happens in films."

She sighs and takes a sip of her cappuccino.

"Don't put so much pressure on yourself. Remember, it's about the rest of your life, not one day. So what if today hasn't gone the way you thought it would? So what if it rains on the day? So what if it doesn't go perfectly? You love Miranda and Miranda loves you and that's all that matters – that, and that there'll be alcohol."

She laughs. "There will *definitely* be alcohol."

"There you go then," I grin, and we clink coffee cups.

"Thanks," she says. "You always know what to say."

"That's what friends are for."

We finish our drinks and I head home to get ready for my date with Max. He takes me to the cinema to see the latest rom-com and holds my hand throughout the entire film, and then we go to an up-market Thai restaurant. Over our meal, I describe my day with Lucy and he tells me about his flying lesson. I picture him in the cockpit, with aviator shades on, looking all sexy and in control, and Vanessa quivers.

"What are you smiling to yourself about? Sometimes you have a *very* naughty look on your face, madam."

"Why, I'm thinking about you, boss," I tell him, looking through my eyelashes at him.

He takes a sip of his wine, and my eyes linger on his full lips as I remember what it's like to kiss them. His eyelids lower and my breath quickens as he stares heatedly at me. Berlin sing *Take My Breath Away* and I feel like I'm about to spontaneously combust.

The waiter chooses that moment to check if our meals are okay, and the tension is broken. We smile at each other as he walks away.

"Tell me about your friends," I say curiously, taking a sip of my own drink.

"Most of them are in Australia, but I have a few golfing buddies here that I meet up with now and then."

"But no one particularly close?"

"Not here."

"Sounds a bit … lonely."

"I work too much to be lonely."

"How do you fit relationships in?"

"With difficulty. I travel a lot, as you've already had evidence of. It makes it hard to form deep relationships."

"Have you had many long-term relationships?"

"Nothing longer than a few months, but I'm hopeful that's about to change."

I smile at this, and Vanessa preens.

We finish our meal, and he drives me home. He kisses me long and hard at my door, before pulling back.

"You'll be the death of me, woman," he growls. "Get yourself inside before I throw you over my shoulder like the caveman I secretly am."

I smirk and Vanessa giggles. I open the door but he pulls me back for another kiss, lifting me off my feet and twirling me around. I laugh exuberantly and he leans back and smiles at me before putting me back on my feet, and then I'm closing the door behind me and leaning back against it, touching my lips and smiling to myself.

Chapter Fifteen

The next few weeks pass in a blur. My mum and dad visit again and this time Mum's moved onto Tarot card reading, which I flat-out refuse to participate in; Tim remains single, which is the longest I've ever known him not to be dating someone; I go dress shopping again with Lucy and she finally decides on the culottes outfit; and I babysit for Jemima and Gideon one Saturday evening – to everyone's surprise, not least my own, the baby only wakes up once, has a bottle of expressed milk and then falls straight back to sleep. Oh, and of course I go on a few more dates with Max, including, to Lucy's delight, to see *La Traviata* (which I told Max I liked so much I almost peed my pants – he didn't get the reference to Pretty Woman, sadly).

One Thursday in mid-March, Max comes into the office to view the ad we've produced for the first time. We sit in the conference room and, as the lights go down, he places his hand on my thigh. I turn to look at him with my eyebrow cocked but he either doesn't notice or deliberately ignores me because his eyes remain glued to the screen. I try to focus on the ad but it's hard when his thumb starts rubbing up and down my leg and Vanessa pants in my ear.

The ad finishes and Max removes his hand as the lights go back up. Everyone looks at him expectantly.

"Perfect," he declares, and there are smiles all round. Max shakes everyone's hand and thanks them, and Tom escorts him to his office to discuss the account and the timeline for production of the series for the brand based on my proposal. The rest of us return to our stations and carry on working, but twenty minutes later I'm surprised by Tom calling me into the office.

I usually feel relaxed around Max now but with Tom present there's a tension in the room between the three of us. I wonder if Max senses it but he gives no indication.

They ask me some questions about the series and I answer confidently. Max looks at me approvingly but Tom maintains a professional mask and I can't tell what he's thinking. I expect Vanessa to bask in Max's approbation but she seems more interested in gaining Tom's attention. *You can't have them both,* I think to her, and she pouts.

When the meeting breaks up, I walk Max to the lift. It's common knowledge now that we're dating, and he openly gives me a peck on the lips before he leaves. I turn expecting to find Tom watching, but his eyes are glued to his computer screen, and he doesn't look up as I walk past.

Mother's Day arrives. On the Friday before, I arranged a 'Guess Whose Mother' competition to raise money for a children's charity. People had to bring in a photo of their mum to be put on a numbered display board then pay an entry fee to guess which mother belongs to which member of staff. The person with the most correct guesses (Evie) won a bottle of champagne. I raised £150.

I head home on the train on the Sunday morning, carrying a bouquet of flowers for my mum. This time, my reserved seat is empty and I sink into it in relief. Vanessa has decided to absent herself. She's around less and less – usually only when Max or Tom is present – and I'm hearing fewer songs. For the first time in over two years, I'm starting to feel less fragile too. I think I have my new role at work and Max to thank for that.

Dad picks me up at the station again. It's a beautiful spring day and we drive with the windows down.

"How are you, darling?" he asks as he drives along the country roads.

"Good, really good," I answer, heartfelt, and he can tell I really mean it. I tentatively tell him that I've started dating someone and I can tell he's pleased for me.

"You'll have to introduce him to us."

"As long as Mum doesn't try a Tarot card reading on him."

"She's moved on from that."

"What to?"

"Life drawing."

I choke. "What – drawing naked people?"

He nods. "She attends classes at the college in town."

"Wow."

"It –"

"Keeps her busy, I know." We chuckle.

When we pull up in front of the house, Mum greets me with a hug and her usual air kisses and I hand her the flowers. I'm taking her for lunch to the local gastro pub, but she insists on showing me her drawings first. I get dragged into the house and there are five or six sketches framed and hanging on the walls. The origami creations are nowhere to be seen.

"I think you get your artistic talent from me," she declares as I examine each drawing. They're actually not bad, if you're into appreciating the form of over-weight, middle-aged men and women. I tell her that they're excellent, and she beams.

She fetches her coat and we walk the twenty minutes to the pub. I tell her about Max, and she actually sheds a tear.

"Oh, don't, Mum – you'll set *me* off," I say shakily, and she sniffs and wipes delicately at her eyes with a tissue that she pulls from her pocket.

We link arms and I spend the rest of the walk telling her about the dates we've been on and how supportive he's been of my career. As soon as she hears that he's the one who spotted my talent, she declares that she likes him already, and we giggle.

We arrive at the pub and have a leisurely lunch. In a hushed voice, I hear all the latest gossip about the vicar and Mrs. Jones, and how one of 'poor Margaret's' dogs swallowed Alan's wedding ring and she had to fish it out of his poop wearing rubber gloves. I tell her about the preparations for Lucy's wedding and show her a photo of her in her chosen wedding outfit. Mum can't understand why she's not in a dress and I roll my eyes and remind her of what year it is.

When we get back, I hang out with Dad in his shed for a

bit. It smells like pipe tobacco and home. He asks me a few questions about Max, then describes the courtship rituals in medieval times (lots of serenading and flowery poetry, apparently), then it's time for him to drop me back at the station.

Max texts when I'm on the train going home.

Did you have a nice time with your mum? x

Lovely, thanks. Did you remember to send flowers to yours? x

I did. What are you doing next weekend? x

No plans as yet x

Keep it free please x

What – the whole weekend?! x

Oui. Do you have a passport? x

Yes …?

A little bird told me it's your birthday soon. You were very naughty for not telling me, madam. We're going to celebrate in style x

Are you saying what I think you're saying? x

;-)

OMG! Really???

Yes! P.S. No pressure x

I don't know what to say! x

That's a first ;-)

Now who's the cheeky one? x

☺

☺

The week drags. I tell Lucy about the trip Max has arranged for my birthday, which is on the following Tuesday, and how nervous I am about spending the weekend with him.

"Just go with what feels comfortable – don't overthink it," she advises, and I decide to do as she says.

Max pulls up in the limo at seven-thirty on Saturday morning. The driver takes my overnight case and opens the door for me and Max greets me with a kiss. The car heads to the airport, where Max's plane is waiting for us.

"Excited?" he asks, and I nod.

He takes my hand and leads me up the steps and onto the luxurious jet which is fitted out in plush cream leather seats and warm cherry wood panelling. A steward greets us with champagne and we take our seats.

"I forgot how rich you are," I tell him drily, and he chuckles.

"That's one of the things I like about you."

"Just one?"

"Are you fishing for compliments, madam?"

"Maybe."

He leans in to me. "I like your lips." He kisses me. "I like your long legs." He kisses me again. "I like how accident-prone you are." I slap his arm and he chuckles, then turns serious and takes my chin in his hand. "I like everything about you." This time the kiss lingers.

The plane takes off and arrives in Paris in just under an

hour. Another limo is waiting for us and it doesn't take long before we're pulling up in front of an elegant hotel. Our bags are carried inside and Max checks us in, then we're heading up to our suite in a very grand lift.

Once we're inside, and while Max is dealing with the bellboy, I take a quick look around. The suite is beautiful, all elaborately ornamental in the rococo style, but that's not what concerns me at the moment. It's only when I spot that there are two bedrooms that I let out the breath I hadn't realised I'd been holding. I take a deep breath, and remember Lucy's advice. *Get a grip, Pip!*

The bellboy is just leaving so I head back over to Max. He stretches out his hands to me and I take them and he pulls me in. "Happy?" he murmurs against my lips.

"Happy," I answer softly.

We take a few minutes to freshen up and unpack our things and then we head back to the limo.

The rest of the day is a whirlwind. We have a guided tour around the Louvre, and I get to see works of art like the *Mona Lisa* and the *Venus de Milo* up close. We eat lunch in a restaurant in the Eiffel Tower, where the views over Paris are breath-taking. Then, in the afternoon, we take a walk along the Seine and explore the shops along the Boulevard Saint Germain. Max buys me a tennis bracelet for my birthday.

He surprises me with dinner and a show at the Moulin Rouge in the evening. We sit in a private balcony and watch the spectacular performance full of sequinned and feathered dancers, stunning sets and fabulous music. Vanessa is in heaven.

The show finishes, and we head back to the hotel in the

limo. I expected to be tired but I'm buzzing from the day and champagne. Max holds my hand on the seat between us and I tell him I've had a wonderful time.

"Better than Julia Roberts in *Pretty Woman?*" he asks teasingly.

"You've been talking to Lucy!"

"She was the little bird I mentioned."

"Wait until I see her!"

He chuckles, and pulls me in for a kiss. Vanessa sighs.

We pull up in front of the hotel and the driver holds the door open for us. Hand in hand, we head into the building and take the lift to our floor. In the suite, Max gives me a lingering kiss and murmurs goodnight against my lips, then we go to our respective rooms.

I get ready for bed in my ensuite, and when I'm done, I get under the covers. However, I'm too restless to sleep. I lie there for a good fifteen minutes debating with myself. Finally, I get up and tip-toe to Max's door. My hand hovers over the knob and I chew my lip and tell myself all the reasons why I shouldn't turn it. I'm there for a couple of minutes before Max's voice makes me jump.

"Are you going to stand out there all night, madam?"

I open the door and peek my head around it. He's sitting up in bed with his arms folded across his bare muscled chest, one eyebrow raised. I bite my lip and stare at him, and he pulls back the covers and pats the bed next to him. I scurry over and jump in, and he cuddles me against his chest.

"That wasn't so hard, was it?" he murmurs against my

hair, and I shake my head.

We sit there like that for a while. He strokes my arm lightly and I inhale his masculine scent. His body is warm and I find myself relaxing against him. He must feel it because he tips my head up and kisses me gently. I respond, and he deepens the kiss. I run my fingers up the nape of his neck and he shudders. Feeling more courageous, I climb onto his lap so I'm straddling him. He inhales sharply and grabs my hips, and the kiss becomes more urgent.

One of the straps of my silky nightdress slides off my shoulder and I leave it. I rub my hands up his chest while we kiss, and he cups my head before lowering his and pulling the other strap down so that my nightdress pools around my waist. He lowers his head and nuzzles my breasts, and I arch my back and savour the long-absent sensation of a man's stubble against my sensitive skin. He looks up at me and asks me in a husky voice if I'm sure. In response, I kiss him. He rolls me over and returns the kiss passionately. I clutch at his powerful shoulders.

He starts working his way down my body and I gasp as he reaches my most intimate place.

We continue like this for what could be hours, or only a few minutes, before he's gazing down into my eyes and sliding into my body. I take a minute to adjust to the unfamiliar sensation, and then he's slowly moving his hips and I'm tilting mine in eager response. The night goes on, broken only by the sounds of our gasps and cries of pleasure, and then we fall asleep in each other's arms.

Chapter Sixteen

He wakes me with a cup of coffee the next morning. I only manage to take one sip and then he's taking it out of my hand and putting it down on the bedside table so he can kiss me. It's cold by the time we finish a repeat of last night's performance.

We cuddle for a bit (yes – he's a cuddler!) and then he reluctantly tells me we need to get up if we're going to make it to Versailles before we return home. I'm tempted to suggest that we skip it, but I'd really like to see the palace and gardens so I get up and head to the shower in my ensuite while he heads into his.

The drive to Versailles takes nearly an hour. When we arrive at the palace, we spend time exploring The Royal Apartments and Hall of Mirrors while listening to the audio guide, then eat a light lunch and venture into the gardens and spend the afternoon wandering around examining the fountains and sculptures hand-in-hand. The early April weather is beautiful, and I thank Max again for bringing me here. He strokes his thumb over my finger and kisses me lightly on the lips.

Before we know it, it's time to head back to the airport.

I'm pleasantly exhausted on the flight home. In fact, I end up falling asleep in the comfortable chair and only wake up when it's time to land. I grimace at the thought that I was drooling in my sleep. Max laughingly tells me that I snore adorably.

Another limo is waiting for us at the airport and Max drops me home before heading back to his place. We smooch on my doorstep, and he tells me to get inside before it's too late.

"Too late for what, boss?" I ask archly.

"You know what, madam." And with another quick kiss he turns and walks back to the limo. I skip up into my flat, smiling.

I meet up with Lucy for lunch the next day. When I start to tell her about our visits to the Louvre, the Eiffel Tower, the Moulin Rouge and Versailles, she waves it all away impatiently.

"Yes, yes – you can tell me about the tourist attractions after. Get to the juicy bit."

I feel my cheeks turn red and smile slyly at her. She claps her hands and squeals.

"And?"

"Heaven."

"Eeek!"

We laugh, and our food arrives.

"I'm so damn pleased for you," she gushes sincerely once

the waitress has gone. She reaches out and clutches my hand and I give it a squeeze.

"Thanks, mate."

During the afternoon, Tom stops by my desk when it's quiet and clears his throat. "How was Paris?"

"Really beautiful," I tell him. He nods and there's an awkward silence. "Have you ever been?" I say into the gap.

"Melanie and I went a few years ago."

"Ah."

He taps my desk but doesn't say anything.

"How is Melanie?"

"She's fine. I think."

My brow furrows. "You think?"

He looks around awkwardly. "We, er, we broke up."

"Oh, I'm so sorry."

He shrugs. "It was coming for a while."

"Still doesn't make it easy, especially after you were together for all that time," I answer sympathetically.

He nods stiffly and taps the desk again. "Well, I'll leave you to your work. I'm glad you enjoyed your trip." And with that, he turns and heads back to his office. Vanessa gazes after him mournfully.

The next day is my birthday, and Max wakes me up with a phone call, then I take time to open the cards that the post man delivers and respond to the text messages that my friends have sent me. There's one from Jemima and a few from old work colleagues and an old school friend who I don't see much anymore. My mum and dad are getting the train down and meeting me straight after work, then we're going for a meal. I was tempted to invite Max, but I don't think I'm quite ready to take that step yet.

I arrive at work to a chorus of 'Happy birthday, Pips!' and Lucy and Tim hug me and present me with a joint gift.

"It's a spa day voucher for two. You're taking me," Lucy informs me excitedly before I even open the envelope. I laugh and give them another hug, and then they head off to get started on their work.

I settle down at my desk at last and continue storyboarding for a new campaign. It's not until mid-morning that I need to open my drawer, and when I do I discover a cream box tied with a pale blue ribbon. I smile and open it, expecting it to be a surprise from Max that he got someone (probably Lucy) to plant there, but when I open it, it's to find a fridge magnet depicting Van Gogh's *Café Terrace at Night* and I know instantly who it's from. Touched, I glance over at Tom's office to find him looking back at me, and I smile and mouth 'Thank you'. He nods expressionlessly and turns to carry on working, and I put the magnet back into its box and slide it into my handbag.

In the afternoon, a bouquet of flowers arrives from Max, with a note saying *Happy birthday, madam. I can't stop thinking about you x*

My mum and dad arrive at reception just before five o'clock. I wave to them and gather my things but when I turn back Tom's already there talking to them. I make my way over.

"Hello, darling, happy birthday!" Dad greets me with a kiss.

"You didn't tell us that Anne Arnold's son was your boss!" my mum admonishes me.

"It must have slipped my mind."

"Well, since you're here, why don't you come for dinner with us, Tom? It can be a thank you for fixing that leaky tap for us," she tells Tom.

I open my mouth to make an excuse for him, but he accepts before I can get the first word out. I look at him in surprise but he doesn't notice as he's already heading to collect his jacket.

"He fixed a leaky tap for you?" I ask in surprise.

"Mmm. I popped around to read his mum's cards last week and he was there. He was fixing a pipe under her sink and I happened to mention that our kitchen tap was leaking so he said he'd pop over to take a look at it. Such a nice young man," she gushes.

"I thought you'd moved onto life drawing," I say, confused.

"Oh, I have, but I'd promised Anne ages ago that I'd do her a reading and I always try to keep my promises."

"She did a reading for me too," Tom says coming up behind me. I jump and he smirks.

"What did your cards say?" I ask, curious despite myself. We start walking over to the lift.

"That he was coming to a great crossroads in his life, I think it was," my mum answers for him.

"And that I had a few big decisions to make," Tom adds.

"What sort of decisions?" I ask, a creeping sense of foreboding coming over me.

"Oh, love, career, the usual," Mum says flippantly. And I stare at him in horror.

"That's not why you split up with Melanie, is it?"

"What? No! Of course not," he frowns. "That had been coming for a while."

"Don't worry." My mum pats him on the arm. "There's an even greater love waiting for you if you're patient, remember."

I look at Tom and he avoids eye contact, his cheeks pinkening, and then the lift arrives and we step in.

"You're not thinking of leaving, are you?" I blurt as the lift descends. "You've only been here six months." The thought makes me feel strangely uneasy.

"Why would I be thinking of leaving?" he asks, confused.

"The cards ..."

He chuckles. "Oh, no. The cards were fun but I wouldn't base any life decisions on them."

"Good. It wouldn't be the same without you." He looks at me and smiles, and I smile back.

Dad starts talking about the jobs people did in medieval

times, and we exit the lift and walk to the restaurant.

I discover that Tom is weirdly knowledgeable about medieval life, and he and my dad talk non-stop about 'bailiffs', 'reeves' and 'serfs'. He sees my look of astonishment and sheepishly explains that he watches The History Channel a *lot*.

We reach the restaurant and get settled at our table and order our starters. I spoke to Mum on the phone on Sunday night, but she asks for more details about my trip with Max. I feel uncomfortable describing my romantic weekend away in front of Tom at first but soon relax as he adds his own experiences of Paris to the conversation.

The food arrives, and we tuck in. Dad gives us a little bit of a history lesson about the French revolution and Tom asks some clever questions that spur him on. I catch Tom's eye at one point during a particularly enthusiastic monologue and he winks at me when my mum and dad aren't looking.

I ask Mum how her life drawing classes are going and Tom uses his art background to discuss technique with her. I've got to admit, he's doing a great job of engaging them about their interests. It makes me feel nervous about introducing them to Max; I'm not sure if he's interested in history or art, and my mum and dad aren't really savvy about business, so I wonder what they'll talk about when they do finally meet. The thought makes me gulp.

We move onto our main course and the conversation still flows. I find myself quietly listening to the conversation, joining in with a laugh here and there, pleased to see someone being so patient and sensitive to my parents' quirks. I watch Tom while he talks, his full lips curving into a smile and his eyes creasing when my dad says something particularly humorous about something obscure that people did hundreds of years ago. He clasps his hands in front of his chin, using them to gesture expressively now and then, and Mum glows at his attention.

He turns suddenly and sees me watching him, and I can't look away from his chocolatey eyes. He blinks slowly and his lids stay down a little as our eyes hold. It's only when my dad clears his throat that I manage to look away. I flush and notice my mum looking between us. I try to cover by pouring some more wine for everyone but, as I reach for the bottle, I accidentally knock it and it wobbles and nearly topples over. I grab at it a split second before Tom does, and his hand closes over mine. I don't look at him, and his hand lingers for a second too long, then he's taking the bottle from me and asking who needs a top-up. I ignore the knowing look that passes between my mum and dad and force myself to think about Max, but it's hard to even picture his face with Tom sitting there looking all sexy and charming the pants off my parents.

Our plates are cleared away; I study the dessert menu like I'm going to be tested on it.

"What's everyone having?" Dad asks eventually, and Tom and I answer 'Eton Mess' at the same time and everyone laughs.

"Great minds think alike," says my dad.

"They *do*," Tom replies, smirking at me and I can't help an answering smile.

The waitress returns and takes our order, then Dad asks about the campaigns we're currently working on so Tom and I talk enthusiastically about some of the projects we're involved in. Soon our desserts arrive, and before I know it, the meal's over and Tom's offering to drive Mum and Dad back to the train station. They accept, and we walk back to the car park by the office and climb into Tom's SUV, my dad in the front next to Tom and me and Mum in the back.

While we're driving, Mum tells us she's thinking of trying aqua aerobics, and Tom mentions that his mum attends a class on Tuesdays. She says she'll phone her and see if she doesn't mind her tagging along, and Tom reassures her that she'd enjoy the company.

We arrive at the station and my dad shakes Tom's hand. I get out to hug them and watch them walk into the station and when I turn back, Tom waves for me to get into the front of the car. As soon as I do, I inhale and smell that tropical aftershave of his and his uniquely masculine scent. I suddenly feel a nervous tension as he guides the car out of the car park.

We sit in silence for a while as he navigates the roads back towards our borough. Then he says, "You know, there's no reason why you should have to get the bus to and from work when we live so close to each other – I could drive you."

I bite my lip before murmuring, "I don't think that's such a good idea, do you?"

"Why not?"

"You know why."

His lips tighten. "I want you to spell it out."

"Why?"

"Because I want you to admit what I admitted to myself

ages ago."

I inhale sharply. "Tom …"

"What?"

"I'm with Max."

"You can't deny what's between us." And I don't respond, because I can't.

We drive the rest of the way in silence and finally we pull up in front of my building.

"I'll wait as long as it takes," he tells me quietly as I push open the car door. I hesitate, and then I'm climbing out and shutting it softly behind me. He waits until I'm through my front door before he drives away.

Chapter Seventeen

Max phones when I get in, to ask how the meal went, but I can hardly concentrate on the conversation. He's in Ireland. As he rings off, he tells me he'll see me on Saturday. I spend the rest of the evening trying to read *Persuasion* but failing dismally.

The rest of the week is a struggle. I can't stop looking over at Tom and it's like I've got a sixth sense because every time I do it's to discover that he's already looking at me. He makes no attempt at trying to hide it and I blush and squirm in my seat. I remember how he said that once he sets his sights on something, he finds it hard not to go after it, and the thought sends heat racing through my body. Fortunately, I don't have any meetings with him. He doesn't send for me once, and I sense that he's trying not to put too much pressure on me – and after all, if I wasn't looking at him, I wouldn't know that he was looking at me, would I reader?

Max calls me every day, telling me he can't wait to see me, and his voice melts me every time. I remember our weekend in Paris, and my pulse quickens. He's persuaded me to go horse riding with him, and Saturday dawns bright and sunny – perfect weather for being outdoors if I wasn't so terrified.

He picks me up at ten in a four-wheel drive, and we head out of town. During the drive, he tells me more about his trip to Ireland and I describe my week in more detail than I went into over the phone, minus any reference to Tom. We discuss progress on the ad series and he seems pleased; as I talk, he takes my hand and raises it to his lips, kissing it gently.

We arrive at the stables after driving for an hour, and he introduces me to the friendly staff as his girlfriend. He hands me a helmet and shows me how to greet the horse, a cob called Buck, which I'm informed is a good, calm horse for beginners. I follow his instructions and extend my arm, offering the back of my hand for the horse to smell and wait for him to touch it, which he does, and I beam. A member of staff holds his head in readiness for me to mount and I hold the reins and Max helps me to position my foot into the stirrup and push myself off the floor and swing my leg over the horse's back. I find myself suddenly astride him, adjusting to the strange sensation of the saddle, with Max grinning up at me.

I put my foot in the other stirrup, and the guide advises me to sit straight but relaxed and hold the reins gently. Max mounts his own horse, which is a lot bigger than mine, and we set off, the guide leading the way along the lane. I learn to allow my body to rock with the motion of Buck as we head out at a steady walking pace along the lane.

There's a slight mist in the air, but the views across the countryside are still pretty amazing. I smile at Max and he winks at me.

We ride for over an hour, then we return. Max helps me dismount and his hands linger on my waist as he nuzzles my neck. "Did you enjoy that?"

"Mmm," I say, patting Buck before he's led away.

"I'm proud of you – you didn't even come close to falling off." I swat him and he chuckles.

I feel a bit wobbly on my feet after being in the saddle, and my inner thighs are a bit sore, but I'm grateful for the experience. Max tells me I'll be cantering before I know it but I'm not sure I'd go that far.

He drives us to a country pub for lunch, and just before we finish, he takes my hand and asks if I want to stay at his place tonight. I bite my lip and nod, and when we're done, he drives back to my flat so I can collect a few necessities before heading over to his house.

I'll leave the rest up to your imagination, reader.

Things settle into a routine. I see Max once or twice every week when he's not jetting off somewhere, and speak to him on the phone most days; I go bridesmaid dress shopping with Lucy and Miranda, and we finally settle on a fitted strapless pale blue silk dress with a fishtail skirt; Tom is back to being Mr. Professional except for the heated look in his eyes when we have to work closely together; and Tim meets a girl online whose name *isn't* the title of a song so Lucy and I decide this one's got potential (she's called Gemma, and she's a nurse, and I can't think of anything smart to say about that, but Lucy slyly tells him that she hopes he gets some *Sexual Healing* and he rolls his eyes).

One day, at the start of May, Max comes into the office to

see the ad for stage one of our new campaign. When the lights go up, it's clear that he's pleased, and he leans over to kiss me in front of everyone. I blush and glance over at Tom, and he's staring back with hooded eyes. I see Max glance at him sharply but Simon comes over to ask him what he thinks of the ad and I think at first that this distracts him. But I see a new, competitive gleam in his eyes when he shakes Tom's hand, which Tom reciprocates, and I cringe inwardly. Vanessa has made a rare appearance and her head swivels between the two as if not knowing who to root for. *Max* I think at her, but her slutty eyes keep straying to Tom. I picture them facing off in a boxing ring going head-to-head, gloves on and gum shields glowing while the *Rocky* theme song plays, and I gulp.

Max places his arm across my shoulder as we exit the conference room and I almost roll my eyes at the possessive gesture. At the lift, he kisses me lingeringly and I blush because I can feel Tom's eyes on us. The doors slide open, and Max enters. He turns around and waits for them to close; as they do, he winks, and then he's gone.

I head back to my desk, refusing to glance in Tom's direction.

Lucy and I go on our spa break that weekend. I have a massage and she has a facial, and then we lounge around the pool for a bit and I finally tell her about Tom's declaration. She gapes as I reveal the details, going back as far as the initial 'Pounds for Kisses' episode and the accidental kiss at the New Year's Eve party, and grins when I tell her about the slap on Valentine's Day.

"You lucky cow," she finally says when I've finished.

"Lucky? It doesn't feel like it."

She cocks an eyebrow. "You've got two gorgeous men lusting after you – one of whom you've had a crush on for *months* and one of whom is a *millionaire*, for God's sake. I'd call that pretty lucky, for a straight woman at least."

I sigh. "I'm with Max now, though."

"True. You can still enjoy the attention though, especially after all the shit you've been through. And after all, it doesn't hurt to look."

"I'm pretty sure Max suspects that Tom likes me."

"Good. It will keep him on his toes. A little competition never hurt anyone."

I realise Lucy's right – it's hardly the most traumatic dilemma in the world to have, as she says, two gorgeous men interested in me. Six months ago, I was single, with only Mr. Fluffles to keep me warm at night, so what the hell am I stressing about?

We decide to grab some lunch, then slip into the Jacuzzi. The heat and the bubbles ease the tension from my tight muscles, and I relax against the side. A few people swim lengths in the pool, and we watch them for a bit. Lucy gets fed up of the heat after a while and gets out and sits on the side, dangling her legs in the water.

"I think we've decided on our sperm donor," she tells me.

"That's brilliant!"

"He's a bio-chemist. He's twenty-nine, six-foot one and

mixed-race like Miranda."

"He sounds perfect."

She bites her lip. "Are you okay about … about me getting pregnant?" she blurts.

I blink in surprise. "Of course! Why wouldn't I be?"

"I just thought it might bring up some bad memories." She looks at me anxiously, and I suddenly realise what she means. I put my hand over hers.

"I'm *completely* happy for you."

She turns her palm up and closes her fingers around mine. "I know you don't like to talk about it, but how old would he be now?" she asks softly.

I take a shaky breath. "Just turned two."

She closes her eyes and squeezes my hand. I squeeze it back, and a tear slips out of my eye, which I brush away.

"Come on, let's go for a swim." She pulls me up and we squeal and jump into the pool with a giant splash. I resurface, gasping, and I feel like I've been baptised. We paddle up and down leisurely, splashing each other occasionally, and Bob Marley sings *Everything's Gonna Be Alright* through the speaker.

That night, we stay awake chatting and giggling across our twin beds until the early hours, and I realise that I feel at peace for the first time in a long time.

The next weekend, I've agreed to babysit for Jemima and Gideon again. I asked Max if he wanted to come with me, but he grimaced and said it was his idea of hell.

I turn up at eight to find Jemima looking much more relaxed than the last time I saw her – the kids are sleeping better and she's taking anti-depressants after Gideon took my advice and persuaded her to go to the GP. I hug them and tell them to stay out as long as they want, then spend the evening watching back-to-back talent shows and eating junk. The baby doesn't wake up once.

The following day, Max takes me to an indoor ski centre. I've never been skiing but I'm feeling pretty confident after the success of bowling and horse riding and so I agree to give it a go. Max has booked me a private forty-five-minute lesson so I get kitted out in the hired salopettes, jacket, gloves, helmet and ski boots. All around me are people who seem to know exactly what they're doing, and I'm surprised at the number of expert snowboarders whizzing around when I get my first view of the main slope. My breath fogs in the chill air and my eyes take a minute to grow accustomed to the whiteness of the snow.

My lesson is on the beginners' slope, and my tutor is called Sam. He helps me to step into my rented skis and I hear a satisfying click as my boots are secured. Then he starts teaching me the basics – how to slow down and stop by pointing the front tips of my skis together while pushing out with my heels to form a wedge shape; how to walk by simultaneously stabbing the poles into the snow and pulling myself forward, keeping my skis parallel; how to side-step up an incline; how to adopt the correct posture for skiing by bending my knees and leaning slightly forwards; and how to turn, fall and get up after a fall. Max watches from the side, dressed in his own ski clothes, and tells me I did well when the lesson is over.

"Ready to have some fun?" he asks with a challenging glint in his eye.

"You bet," I tell him confidently.

He clicks on his skis and we get to the top of the slope.

"Ready?" he says, as we're poised at the top.

"Ready!" I say, and push off before he does. I hear him laugh and shout "Cheat!" behind me, but he soon overtakes me and glances back as he passes, grinning in victory. I swear and speed up, trying to catch him, but someone gets in my way and I swerve to avoid them. In my panic, I forget everything that Sam taught me and fall over in exactly the wrong way. As I do, I feel something snap and an excruciating pain explodes in my lower leg. I scream and slide to a stop.

Max rushes over to me and I wincingly tell him I think I've broken my right leg. There's a bustle of first-aiders, and I end up in hospital being X-rayed, where the doctor confirms what I suspect. Max stays with me the whole time, and I leave hours later with a plaster cast on and crutches.

He helps me into the car, and I look up at him sheepishly. He shakes his head in exasperation and bends further in to kiss me softly on the lips. Then he's shutting the door and walking around to the driver's side so he can take me home.

Max offers to stay the night with me but I say I'll be fine. In fact, I'm exhausted, so after helping me to get settled in, he kisses me goodbye and heads home, making me promise that I'll call if I need anything before he'll leave. The painkillers they gave me at the hospital are doing their work, and I fall asleep almost as soon as Max has left.

I don't wake up until eight the next morning, when Max phones to check on me. I call into work and tell Jean what's happened and that I'll be taking a few days off and she promises to pass the message on. I text Lucy and my mum and dad, then cautiously get out of bed and clumsily stand up using my crutches for support. Awkwardly, I manage to make myself a simple breakfast of porridge and juice, and sit watching daytime TV for the morning.

Lucy texts back, telling me she'll be round after work to help me with anything I need, and Mum and Dad call, offering to come and look after me, but I tell them I have friends helping and can manage and they reluctantly agree to stay at home. I also get a text from Tom.

Max pops in at lunchtime and makes me a sandwich, but he has to head off to a meeting so he only stays for half an hour.

Lucy arrives at six with a take-away. While we eat on trays in the living room, I tell her that Max came around and she makes another *Sexual Healing* joke. I roll my eyes and tell her that's the last thing on my mind at the moment. We finish eating and then she helps me to have a shower before she heads home.

After three days of daytime TV, and quick visits from Max and Lucy, I'm thoroughly fed up. I've been practising on my crutches and I decide that there's no reason why I can't go into work. I book a taxi, though, the walk to the bus stop being more than I can handle, and get up extra early on Thursday morning so I have enough time to get ready. I put the radio on while I go through my routine and Donna Summer sings *She Works Hard for the Money* and I bop along as best I can.

The taxi arrives and I carefully make my way downstairs and get into the vehicle. The driver has kindly got out and opened the door for me and I thank him gratefully as I fall back against the seat. We spend the journey discussing how I broke my leg, and before I know it, we've arrived at work. I pay him and he helps me out, making sure I'm stable on my crutches before he gets back in, and I slowly make my way into the building. I thank the Lord for lifts as I make my way up to the correct floor.

Chapter Eighteen

Jean does a double-take when I step out of the lift, and I grin at her surprise. As soon as my work colleagues see me, they bustle around me, settling me into my chair and admonishing me for coming in when I should be resting. I tell them I'm fine.

"Have you seen daytime TV lately?" I ask with an arched eyebrow, and they chuckle.

They part like the Red Sea when Tom arrives. He doesn't look very happy.

"My office. Now," he barks, and I grimace. I get up clumsily using my crutches, and he swears and scoops me up before carrying me like a bride into his office. I look back to see my colleagues staring after us, and I mouth 'Help!' to them but none of them move. Lucy actually grins and gives me a thumbs up.

He uses his shoulder to open his office door and leans back against it to close it. Then he stops and looks down at me with a tight mouth.

"What do you think you're playing at?" he asks me in a controlled manner. I look up at him sheepishly.

"I was bored."

He lets out an exasperated sigh. "As much as it's nice to see you, you should be at home resting."

"I can rest in my chair here and get some work done at the same time. It's win-win." I give him my best hopeful, puppy-dog eyes, and I see him relenting.

We stay like that for some moments before I finally ask if he's going to put me down. He's still standing with his back to the door.

He tightens his grip and looks down at me slyly. "Why would I? I have you exactly where I want you."

I feel my cheeks flush, and his eyes glitter down at me. My heart starts pounding and I feel heat gathering low in my abdomen. We stare at each other, and I feel a sensation that's very close to disappointment when we're interrupted by a knock on the door. It's Tim, checking to see how I am; he was on the phone when I arrived. He gives me an awkward hug and looks at Tom in bemusement. Reluctantly, Tom crosses the office and lowers me into a chair by his desk. Tim starts chattering away about one of his accounts and I see Tom start to grow impatient. He gives short, clipped answers and puts his hands on his hips, but Tim is oblivious and carries on as if he has all the time in the world.

Finally, after what seems like hours, Lucy knocks on the glass door and tells him there's a client on the phone for him. He takes his leave and Lucy winks at me before she follows behind him. Tom is heading around his desk to his chair and doesn't see. He sits opposite me, steepling his hands against his chin and looking across at me with hooded eyes.

"What am I going to do with you, madam?" he asks, and his unwitting use of Max's nickname for me makes me blush with shame at my earlier reaction to him, but I can't help answering coyly.

"What would you *like* to do with me, sir?"

He inhales sharply and his lids lower even further. "Let's just say that my palm's twitching, madam." And I hear panting in my ear as Vanessa returns after a long absence. My cheeks turn redder, and I bite my lip as I remember the slap at bowling. *50 Shades eat your heart out*, I think.

"Is it hot in here, or is it me?" I finally ask softly, fanning myself, and the tension is broken as he laughs.

"What have you been up to the last few days? I wanted to visit, but I understand Lucy's been around every night, and I assume Max has been helping you," he finishes awkwardly.

"Lucy's been great. I've been watching a lot of TV. Max popped around the first couple of days but he's in America now – a business trip he couldn't cancel," I tell him, equally awkwardly.

"Ah. Have you been eating okay?"

"Lucy's brought a takeaway each night," I cringe.

"Twenty-seven and fifty-three?" he smirks, and I laugh.

"Nope."

"Pity. Good spring rolls." And I roll my eyes but smile as he repeats my words back to me.

A thought suddenly occurs to him. "How did you get here today?"

"Taxi."

"That'll cost you a fortune!" he says in outrage.

I shrug. What other choice did I have? "I can afford it."

He frowns sceptically. "How? We don't pay you *that* much."

"Insurance policy pay-out," I answer simply, and that makes him pause.

"Well, even so, there's no need for you to waste money getting taxis to and from work for however many weeks you'll be in that thing. I can drive you."

I open my mouth to protest but he holds his hand up. "I won't take no for an answer." And I snap my mouth closed.

Simon arrives at the door then, and Tom reluctantly hands me my crutches and watches me leave the office like an anxious parent. I arrive back at my desk and settle down to work.

Five o'clock rolls around before I know it and Tom arrives at my desk and helps me into my jacket. I refuse his sly offer to carry me and we make our way slowly to the lift. I wait on a bench outside the office, basking in the mid-May sun while he collects the car and brings it around to the front of the building.

The ride home is relaxed, and we spend most of it talking about work. When we arrive outside my building, he gets out to help me into the flat, taking my key from me to open the door and then scooping me up again to carry me up the stairs. He places me gently down on the sofa and leans my crutches at the side of me.

"Thanks for the lift," I tell him, then add awkwardly, "Do you want to stay for a coffee or anything?"

He looks tempted, but then says that he can't. "I'm going to my sister's – her husband's away and she's struggling with post-natal depression."

"Oh, I'm so sorry," I answer sympathetically and tell him about Jemima.

"It's more common than people realise," he sighs.

"Jemima seems to be coming out of it now – hopefully your sister will too."

He nods. "Anyway, I'd better go." He hesitates, sneaks a quick peck on the cheek, and then he's out the door and bounding down the stairs. I get up and shove a meal into the microwave, then spend the evening trying to read *Sense and Sensibility,* only to be interrupted by a call from Max. He's concerned that I've gone back to work but I tell him that I was going stir-crazy.

"You're a stubborn madam," he answers in exasperation, and his use of my nickname makes me feel guilty as I remember the earlier exchange with Tom. But it was only a bit of harmless flirting … wasn't it?

We chat about work for a bit before ringing off, and I end up tossing and turning for half the night.

Tom and I fall into a comfortable routine. He collects me each morning at a quarter past eight and he maintains a friendly but professional dialogue all the way to work and on the return journey. I get to know him better and I've got to say that I'm delighted to discover that he plays 60s, 70s and 80s music in his car. We often sing along and smile at each other in rueful acknowledgement of how uncool we are.

Max returns from his business trip and I can tell that he's not best pleased that Tom's giving me lifts, but he doesn't say anything. We go out on more dates, and I stay over at his house most weekends, and we grow more and more comfortable with each other – so much so that I decide it's time to introduce him to my mum and dad. I do so on the weekend before Lucy and Miranda's wedding.

We drive over one Sunday at the start of June and meet them at the gastro pub where I took my mum on Mother's Day. Max shakes my dad's hand firmly and looks him in the eye, and I can tell that first impressions are good. However, it soon goes downhill fast. We settle down and look over the menus, and while we do so, Mum starts gushing about her latest hobby – genealogy. She reckons she's traced our family line back to a 17th century duke, which means that we're related to royalty. I hear Max snort quietly and I cover quickly by asking a question about what else she's discovered, but I suspect Mum heard because she tries to hide a hurt look. Dad is oblivious and soon starts asking about Max's family tree. I think we're on safe ground as he gives a brief overview of his parents and grandparents, but Dad can't resist a history lesson on the first Australian settlers.

"It was Captain Arthur Philip who took the first convicts to Sydney Cove in 1788. Within ten years, the indigenous population was reduced by *ninety* percent. It wasn't just the new diseases that they faced – the expansion of British colonies over the next few decades resulted in competition for land and resources. The indigenous people were massacred – hunted down and shot en masse, even driven off cliffs. A terrible time in history – your ancestors may very well have been involved, Max," he finishes innocently, and I see Max grimace. I down my glass of wine and hurry to change the subject. Desperate, I ask Mum if she's still going to aqua aerobics, but she must still be sulking because her lips are pursed and she just gives a curt nod and I'm forced to dig deep to keep the conversation flowing. I breathe a sigh of relief when the waitress arrives.

When she leaves, Dad asks Max about his work, and Max explains his business and what it involves day-to-day. My parents don't really have any sense of or interest in the world of commerce, and it's soon clear that their attention is slipping. Panicking, I inject the story of when I turned up late and fell into the meeting and exposed my tucked-in skirt. Dad chuckles and Mum manages a small smile, but Max pats me on the head and calls me a 'clumsy so-and-so', and though he means it affectionately, I see my dad frown at him. I pour everyone (except Max) another glass of wine and pray that the alcohol helps to smooth things out. To be honest, it doesn't help that Paul McCartney is singing *Hope of Deliverance* over the speakers.

Our food arrives, and we all dive into it gratefully. There's a long silence while we eat, and I struggle to think of something safe to talk about. I finally fall back on our trip to Paris, describing the views from the Eiffel Tower in more detail than I think they've ever been described in the history of French tourism.

"Speaking of convicts," my dad interjects, and my heart

sinks as I see Max's lips tighten and Dad starts a monologue about the storming of the Bastille in 1789.

We all decide to skip dessert and I feel a mixture of relief and disappointment as we head out to the car park. I kiss my parents goodbye and Dad shakes Max's hand again but mum barely acknowledges him. We each head to our respective cars.

Max and I don't speak as we click our seatbelts in and he turns on the ignition before reversing out of the space and heading out onto the road that will take us back to London. After five minutes of silence, I sigh and see his hands tighten on the steering wheel. I finally decide to break the tension.

"Well, that could have gone better."

"A lot better."

"My dad didn't mean to be rude."

"And yet he was," he says through tight lips.

"Well, you were too," I frown.

"How?"

"You snorted at my mum's research."

He snorts now. "Well, it's highly unlikely that you're descended from royalty."

"I know that, but you could have humoured her."

"Why? I haven't got where I am today by humouring people."

I take a breath. "Yes, but this isn't business, is it? This is my family."

He's silent at this, and I decide to let the subject drop. Huey Lewis and the News start singing *Trouble in Paradise* and

Max turns the radio off. We don't talk for the rest of the drive back.

When we arrive outside my building, I give him a perfunctory kiss on the cheek and hop out of the car. He waits for me to go inside and then he drives away.

Max texts me later that night.

Sorry if I was rude to your mum. Maybe we can try again. Friends? x

Friends x

See you Wednesday x

xxx

Chapter Nineteen

The next few days pass without incident. Tom still drives me to and from work and I keep working on stage two of our ad series for Max, as well as a few other projects. I go out for lunch with Tim and Lucy and all of the talk is about the hen party (which is on Thursday and will be comprised of a mixture of male and female friends, Lucy and Miranda being anything but conventional) and the wedding, which is on Saturday. We've all booked Friday off work so we can recover from the night before. Tim is bringing Gemma to the wedding, and Lucy and I tell him that we can't wait to meet her. He's been less starry-eyed this time, and taking things at a reasonable pace, though we can tell that he's really into her. Lucy thinks he's finally grown up, and I think she might be right.

On Wednesday, Tom has arranged for us to take Max clay-pigeon shooting. It's one of those 'schmooze-the-client' days and a group of us who've been working on his account have been invited. I'm still on crutches, but Tom and Max have both insisted that I tag along. They promise me a chair, and I reluctantly agree.

Tom drives us to the range in the morning, and Max arrives not long after. I discover that they're both experienced shooters, and (surprise, surprise) I see the competitive gleam in their eyes as they greet each other and shake hands, their grips firm. There's an instructor for those of us who are new to the sport, but I decide not to participate. Even if I could balance properly to shoot, I'm not sure that anyone around me would be safe if I was allowed to wave a gun around. And if not someone else, I'd probably end up accidentally shooting myself in my good foot and end up having to wheel myself down the aisle at Lucy's wedding.

We have a safety briefing and guns are selected for those taking part. Ear defenders and eye protection is distributed and we're good to go.

The views over the open countryside are beautiful, and I sit under a shelter watching as the others take turns aiming and firing at the clay pigeons as they shoot out into the air, and the instructor gives tips and advice. Of course, Tom and Max hit every target, and I give them both the thumbs up each time they look back at me to check if I'm witnessing how amazing they are. I roll my eyes at Simon behind their backs, and he shakes his head in amusement.

I sit by Max for lunch, though I spend most of it talking to other members of the team while he's engaged by Tom and Simon. There's still a slight tension between us from our tiff over the weekend, but this isn't the right circumstance to iron things out, and Max has to leave for another meeting not long after we finish eating. He gives me a quick peck on the lips, and then he's gone. I turn to find Tom waiting patiently to drive us back, his face carefully schooled into one of nonchalance. He keeps pace with me as we follow behind the others, but neither of us speaks.

Thursday evening arrives and I rush home from work to shower and get ready for the hen party. Max has arranged a limo for us and I clamber awkwardly into it when it arrives and then head over to Lucy and Miranda's place. I get there to find that most of the guests have already arrived – there are sixteen of us in total, including close family and friends. Tim is the last one to show up, and I greet him with a glass of champagne and we all toast to a fabulous night for the happy couple.

I look at my watch and hurry everyone into the limo which is waiting outside, and we head to the club. The mood on the journey is jubilant, everyone is talking at once and drinking more champagne, and Lucy and Miranda sit close together and smile at the happy chaos.

We arrive and scramble out, and I confirm the pick-up time with the driver before heading inside. We get escorted to our table and several jugs of alcohol quickly arrive. The room is already half-full and more guests are being led in all the time. The noise level rises as the room fills and an air of anticipation fills the large, opulent space.

Soon, the lights dim and the hostess-compère arrives on the stage to tumultuous applause. It's a drag act, and we're all soon belly-laughing and whooping at the sassy and witty comments, and cheering as she congratulates some of the 'special guests' of the evening, including Miranda and Lucy. We whistle as she starts performing songs, which range from *The Lady is a Tramp* to *Sisters Are Doing It for Themselves*. It's a full-on cabaret act, with chorus 'girls' and more sequins and feathers than I've seen outside of the Moulin Rouge. *Vanessa would love this*, I think, but I hardly see her any more.

We soon reach the intermission, and we're served a two-course meal at our tables. I check in with Lucy and Miranda, and they hug me as they thank me for organising the evening and gush about what a fabulous time they're having. I hug them back and tell them how pleased I am.

The second half starts, and it's even more elaborate than the first. We sing along with each performance, and lots of people get out of their seats to bop away. I wave my crutches in the air in lieu of dancing, and get a cheeky comment from the drag queen.

The show builds to its climax, and the performers get a standing ovation from the audience. The dance floor is cleared and a disco starts, and I'm pulled up to join everyone. I sway in time to the music while leaning on my crutches, watching Lucy and Miranda beam as they boogie with their nearest and dearest. Eventually, I have to sit down, and I smile as the DJ switches to slow songs and the happy couple start smooching.

Tim draws my attention, and we chat drunkenly about subjects that range from weddings to the best way to eat a Kit Kat (don't get me started, reader!). As the DJ finally announces the last song of the night, Tim looks at me curiously.

"There's a rumour going around the office," he tells me.

"Oh? I haven't heard anything."

"People are saying that Tom's got a crush on you – that he made it pretty obvious on the clay pigeon shoot."

"Oh."

"It's true then?"

I shift uncomfortably on my seat. "Well ..."

"I had no idea!"

I think back to the day when I returned to work and Tim came into Tom's office when Tom was holding me like a bride, and stop myself from rolling my eyes and smiling at his endearing obliviousness.

I shrug instead. "It's irrelevant – I'm with Max now." Let's forget that things have been a bit cool between us since he met my mum and dad.

"That's a shame – you were *really* into Tom before Christmas."

My cheeks redden. "I know."

Lucy's brother attracts Tim's attention from the other side, and he turns to chat with him. I sit watching the dancers and brooding.

The disco finishes, and Lucy and Miranda and a few of the others make their way back to our table. We finish our drinks, and I call the limo driver to make sure that he's arrived. The return journey is quieter; everyone seems tired but content, and more than a little soporific due to the consumption of a *lot* of alcohol. We drop off a few people on the way back to Lucy and Miranda's flat, and soon there's just the three of us left, plus Lucy's brother and sister-in-law, who are sleeping over. They all hug me as the limo arrives at their building and they start getting out, and Lucy sheds a few tears as she slurringly tells me I'm 'the betht friend ever'. Miranda and I laugh as she lisps and Miranda steadies her as she exits the vehicle and they make their way inside.

The driver drops me home, and I get out and thank him as he holds the door open for me. Once I'm inside, I check my phone. I have one message. I open it, expecting it to be from Max, but it's from Tom hoping that we all had a good evening. I send a quick reply, then get ready for bed. I fall immediately into a dreamless sleep.

The next day is Friday, and I spend half of it in bed recovering from a killer hangover and eventually getting round to packing my bag for the weekend while Mr. Fluffles weaves around my crutches. Max is picking me up at ten in the morning and the wedding is at three. He calls me at half-past four.

"I'm really sorry, but I've got a problem I need to deal with in Germany. I'm just about to head to the airport. I won't make it back in time for the wedding."

"Ha ha, very funny, Max."

There's a pause. "No, I'm serious."

"Oh. Right. Er … I don't know what to say. I guess you have to do what you have to do."

"If there was a way that someone else could go in lieu, or if it wasn't so urgent —"

"I get it. It's fine. I'll, erm, give your apologies to Lucy and Miranda."

"Thanks. I really am sorry, sweetheart," he says softly.

"I know."

"I'll still send the car for you at ten and it will drop you back on Sunday – just tell the driver what time you'll want collecting."

"Okay, thanks," I murmur. "Hope you manage to sort the crisis out."

"Me too." And I hear the grimace in his voice.

We exchange goodbyes and hang up, and I sigh and finish packing my bag. I spend a restless night stewing over Max putting business before my best friend's wedding, and then feeling guilty for not being more understanding of the huge responsibility he has on his shoulders. I finally fall asleep properly at four a.m. and my last thought is that I'm going to need to a *lot* of concealer tomorrow.

Unsurprisingly, I oversleep on Saturday morning and end up falling over in my rush to get showered and ready before the car arrives. "I'm fine, I'm absolutely fine!" I tell no one as I stand up on one leg and hop to pick up my crutches from where they fell. Vanessa would be rolling her eyes at me, but the hussy has completely vanished from my life by this point. I feel a weird mixture of relief and sadness at this, but I don't have time to dwell on it because the intercom buzzes and the driver announces that he's here with the car. I manoeuvre carefully down the stairs with my bags slung over my back and open the door. Gratefully, I hand over the holdall and dress bag and follow the driver to the car.

The journey takes just over an hour, during which time I get a text from Max hoping that the wedding goes well and apologising once again. I reply saying that I hope he's not having to sort out anything too stressful, but he doesn't respond.

Lucy comes running out of the hotel when the car pulls up, and I get out. We squeal and hug and then I get checked in and drop my things into my room before heading to hers for lunch and to get ready. Miranda has a different room to prepare in, and then they're in the bridal suite for the night. Room service bring champagne and a tray of delicate sandwiches and pastries, and we sit munching them with her mum and sister while we wait for the hair and makeup lady to arrive.

She arrives at half twelve with an assistant and sets to work. Over the next few hours, we gossip and laugh as Lucy's Mum and sister recount stories from Lucy's childhood – including the time that she was five and a boy kissed her for the first time and she burst into tears. I've made a playlist especially for the occasion and we have it on in the background. It includes everything from Katy Perry's *I Kissed a Girl* to *She* by Elvis Costello. We sing along as we get ready, and even the stylist and her helper join in.

When my hair and makeup are done, I decide to go and check in on Miranda. She's in a room on the other side of the hotel with her own mum, auntie and a friend that she's known since they were at school together, plus her own stylist. I knock on the door and her auntie opens it. We hug and I go in. Miranda is in the process of getting her own hair coiffed so I give her the thumbs up and accept another glass of champagne from her mum.

"How are you feeling?" I ask as I perch on the bed.

"Nervous," she answers. "But the alcohol is helping.

How's Lucy doing?"

"Great – she's excited more than anything." I recount a few of the stories that her mum and sister have shared, including a few that Miranda didn't know, and we laugh at some of her crazy antics.

"And *that's* the woman I love," Miranda declares as I finish telling the story about when Lucy streaked onto a rugby pitch for a dare and got arrested.

I finish my champers, then decide it's high time I was heading back to my BFF. I grab my crutches and give air kisses goodbye so we don't spoil each other's make-up.

"Good luck, my lovely," I tell Miranda, clasping her hand. She takes a deep breath and nods. I squeeze. "It'll all be fine. You look beautiful." She smiles and I make my way to the door.

I'm about half-way back to Lucy's prep room and just passing my own door when someone comes out of the room next to mine and nearly bumps into me. I wobble and manage to stop myself from toppling over just in time, then blink as I realise that it's Tom. He looks startled but reaches out to steady me. I murmur, "Thanks," and he reluctantly drops his hand.

"We must stop bumping into each other like this," I attempt to joke, and one side of his mouth curves up.

"*All the better to sexually harass you, my dear,*" he answers in a deep voice. I burst out laughing and he leans against the door.

"Aren't you supposed to be dressed by now?"

"I'm saving the dress until the last minute. Knowing me

I'll spill something on it or fall over and rip it if I put it on too soon."

"Very true," he says drily, and I poke him with one of my crutches. He chuckles.

I explain that I've just been to see Miranda and we chat a bit about how they're both doing. Then he looks at me curiously. "I haven't seen Max yet."

"Oh, er, he's not coming. He's been called away on urgent business in Germany."

"That's too bad," he murmurs with lowered eyelids but he doesn't sound too disappointed to be honest, reader.

"Well," I say after a pause. "I'd best be getting back to Lucy."

"Of course."

I make my way past him. When I get to the end of the corridor, I look back. He's still watching me. I give him a small smile, and he nods. *Damn, he looks gorgeous in that suit,* I think as I turn the corner.

Chapter Twenty

I return to the room and report back that Miranda's doing well, albeit a little nervous. Billy Idol is singing *White Wedding* and it's nearly time to head downstairs to the Grand Hall where the ceremony is being held. Lucy's sister helps me to get changed and tie white ribbons and sprigs of flowers to match the bouquets onto my crutches, and we start the ten-minute countdown.

Lucy gulps down the last of her champagne, and we do last-minute hair and makeup checks before we say goodbye to the stylist and her assistant. I give her one last hug. "I'd say 'break a leg' but …" I murmur to her, and she chuckles.

Lucy's dad arrives then and starts crying when he sees her in her bridal outfit, and her mum tells him off for starting her off too and risking her ruining her makeup. We all laugh, and Lucy takes a deep breath, and then we're heading out the door.

Miranda and Lucy have decided to walk down the aisle together, and the former's already waiting outside the Grand Hall when we arrive. She's wearing a beautiful white fitted dress with an A-line skirt. They both exclaim and rush to hug each other, and there's more than a few of us with tears in our eyes. We laugh and hurry to check each other's make up, and then most of the party head inside to take their seats.

The three of us hold hands in a circle and take some deep breaths, then I'm wishing them luck as the music starts playing and I begin to make my way ahead of them down the aisle. People turn and smile at me as Shania Twain sings *From This Moment On* and I swing myself carefully through the centre of the congregation. There are already a few people patting at their eyes and Lucy and Miranda haven't even started down the aisle yet. I can tell when they do because all but one head swivel back to look behind me. I catch Tom's eye and he's staring at me like he's never seen me before. His face is flushed and I've never seen his dark eyes so intense. I inhale sharply and falter and I can't look away, not until I force myself to look where I'm going so I don't ruin my friends' moment by falling over in the middle of the aisle and creating an embarrassing scene.

I arrive where I'm supposed to be and turn to watch Lucy and Miranda as they walk hand-in-hand down the last section of the aisle, stopping before the registrar. I can feel Tom's eyes on me, and I feel that heat return. If Vanessa were here, she'd be panting loudly in my ear. I deliberately don't look at him and focus on concentrating all of my attention on what the lady is saying as she starts the ceremony. Her words are beautiful, and I find myself tearing up. Someone passes me a tissue – I don't see who – and I blot my eyes and try to hold back a full-on blubber session.

We soon reach the vows, which Miranda and Lucy wrote themselves, and they make promises to each other which include everything from always being a shoulder to cry on to taking turns putting the recycling bins out. The congregation laugh at some of the more humorous promises, and I catch Tom's eye at one point and we smile at each other. Everyone cheers when the marriage is officially declared, and Lucy and Miranda kiss. The photographer clicks away, and they move to sign the register with their witnesses: Lucy's sister and Miranda's aunt. And before I know it, they're walking back up the aisle while confetti is thrown like a shower of colourful raindrops.

We congregate outside on the patio in the beautiful June sunshine where people take turns to congratulate the happy couple. A waiter circulates with champagne and orange juice and the photographer starts to get organised for the shots that Miranda and Lucy have asked for. There's woodland around the hotel grounds, and a stream surrounded by weeping willows with a pretty bridge over it, and we spend well over an hour posing for various shots, as well as being caught in more than a few candid ones. I know most of the guests, either from work or from meeting family members over the years of knowing Miranda and Lucy, so I'm never short of company when I'm not required for a photo. I even get to meet Tim's girlfriend, Gemma, at last, and I'm pleased to discover that she seems completely normal, not shallow/vain/selfish/lazy/ bitchy (cross out as appropriate) at all. I give Tim a thumbs up when she's not looking, and he grins.

No matter where I am or who I'm with, though, I always seem to know where Tom is, like he's got a homing beacon attached to his head or something. At one point, he disappears inside, only to reappear several minutes later with two glasses. He heads towards me and tells me I look thirsty as he hands me one. I take a sip, and to my delight it's a

G&T. I look at him in surprise.

"You've been paying attention."

"To you? Always."

I blush and look away. Fortunately (or not), Simon and Evie join us, and I'm soon called for another photo. Tom takes my glass for me, and I go and join Lucy and Miranda on the bridge. When I get back, Tom secures a chair for me and I sink into it gratefully.

We're called inside the marquee to take our seats for the wedding breakfast when the outside photos are done, and I sit on the top table with the brides and their close family. I notice that Tom is seated next to Miranda's beautiful cousin, Grace, and feel a pang of jealousy which I quickly try to squash.

A sumptuous three course meal is served by waiters and waitresses dressed in smart black and white outfits, and I'm soon distracted by the food and lively conversation with the rest of the bridal party. The time for the speeches arrives, and both fathers give heartfelt and often humorous deliveries, and we raise our glasses more than once to the beautiful brides.

The guests mingle while the marquee is rearranged for the evening party, and I find myself in a group with Tom. We grab a table when the room is ready, and people are soon dancing and drinking heavily, especially once the evening guests arrive. Laughter and loud conversation fill the space, and I smile and wave to Lucy and Miranda as they circle the tables after their romantic first dance to Lionel Richie and Diana Ross's *Endless Love*, after which there wasn't a dry eye in the house.

Tom fetches me another G&T and I ask him mock-sternly if he's trying to get me drunk.

"Now there's an idea," he answers, wiggling his eyebrows. I can't help but laugh, but I remind myself about Max, and decide to ease back on the drink. After a while, I check my phone, but there's just an earlier text from my mum and dad, hoping that the wedding goes well.

By ten thirty the hog roast is over and most of the guests are on the dance floor – I'd say half are more than a little drunk. Tom and I are the only ones left at our table, and he surprises me by standing suddenly and holding out his hand.

"Dance with me."

I raise my eyebrows and gesture to my crutches, and he reaches down and scoops me off my chair and starts carrying me onto the dance floor before I can even squeal. People cheer as we join them, and he lowers my legs carefully and I lean against him for support and he starts swaying to and fro to the music.

"Why are you always carrying me around like some kind of caveman?" I enquire tartly, and he chuckles low in my ear.

"Why am I always having to rescue you, like some kind of damsel in distress?" he asks, quirking an eyebrow, and I pull a face. He smiles and holds me tighter. I breathe in his unique scent and find myself relaxing in his arms just as the slow songs start. The Moody Blues croon *Nights in White Satin* and we lapse into silence, swaying gently to the music. I see Lucy watching us as she dances with Miranda and she winks when she notices me looking back. I take a deep breath and look away, but I just get a lungful of Tom and my brain starts to fog. As the song draws to an end, he turns his head and his lips brush against my ear.

"I'm still waiting for you," he murmurs, and I almost turn to jelly. I lean my head against his shoulder, and he wraps his arms further around me. We dance without speaking for the rest of the evening, and Max doesn't enter my mind once.

I look up in surprise when the last song finishes and the lights go up. There are only a few couples left on the dance floor, and the room is half empty. I take a peek up at Tom to find him staring down at me with those hooded eyes of his, and I bite my lip. We're interrupted by Lucy.

"Excuse me, Tom, but I just need a word with my bridesmaid," she says, widening her eyes at me and pulling me away. She takes me over to a corner and starts talking when she's sure no one is around.

"Do you know what you're doing?" she says to me in a hushed voice.

"I have no idea," I answer helplessly.

"I know I said to enjoy being lusted after by two gorgeous men, but I don't want you to do anything you'll regret in the morning."

I nod. "You're right. Good call for pulling me away from the pheromones."

"How much have you had to drink?"

"More than I should have but not as much as I could have."

"Jesus!"

"It's okay. Honestly, I'm okay. I won't do anything I'll regret."

"Promise?"

"Promise."

She looks at me doubtfully, and Miranda comes over and joins us.

"Ready?" she asks her new wife, and she opens her mouth as if to answer in the negative but I wave her away.

"Go – enjoy the start of your honeymoon," I tell her. "Don't worry about me."

She hesitates, then hugs me. "I love you, mate."

"Love you too," I tell her and they make their way towards the exit, where I notice Tom is chatting with a few of our work colleagues. He looks over at me as Lucy and Miranda walk past, and I take a breath and head over to join them.

We step out into the cool night air, and it clears my head a bit as the group makes its way back over to the main building. Everyone else is chatting, some still quite lively, some almost in a stupor; Tom and I are the only silent ones.

As we make our way into the hotel and up in the lift, people gradually peel off to their floors until just Tom and I are left. We finally arrive at our floor and exit the lift and start heading along our corridor. When we reach his door, I carry on past him to mine. We stand outside our rooms, looking across at each other for several moments before he speaks.

"Sleep tight, sweetheart."

"You too."

And then we're both opening our doors and shutting them softly behind us. I lean back against mine and take a shaky breath, then I start getting myself ready for bed in the too-warm hotel room. I lay awake unable to sleep for what seems like hours, knowing that he's just on the other side of the wall.

In the morning, I shower and join the other guests for breakfast. Lucy and Miranda come down soon after, and while Miranda talks to her parents, Lucy rushes over to me where I'm loading up my plate at the hot buffet counter.

"Well?" she hisses excitedly as she grabs two plates and starts piling bacon on to them.

"Well, what?" I answer in mock-confusion.

She huffs in frustration. "You know what! Spit it out — what happened last night?"

"Well, I had a terrible sleep — these rooms are *way* too warm for my liking," I answer with my tongue in my cheek.

Over her shoulder, I notice Tom enter the room and I feel my cheeks blush. Lucy looks behind her and spots him, then turns back to me with a gleam in her eye and that shit-eating grin that she has when something titillates her.

"You *did*, didn't you? Oh my God, I knew it!"

"No! Nothing happened. We said 'goodnight' and went our separate ways — I swear."

She looks closely at my face, and her shoulders slump. "Well, shit, I thought I predicted that one right. I owe Miranda a tenner."

"What? You were the one who said not to do anything I'd regret!"

"I know but you might just as easily have regretted *not* doing anything."

I open my mouth then snap it closed. She has a point.

"I *was* tempted," I admit quietly, looking around covertly to see if anyone's within hearing shot.

"I *knew* it!" she says *way* too loudly for my liking; I hush her.

"But it wouldn't be fair to Max," I point out, and she frowns and nods.

"Gosh, what a dilemma."

"Not really," I lie. "I'm with Max."

"I know, but …"

"But what?"

"You and Tom looked so *right* together last night."

I glance over at him where he's chatting to Mike, and he seems to sense my gaze on him because he turns and looks over at me.

"Holy shit," Lucy breathes. "You're like two magnets."

I smile at Tom politely and he smiles back, then I turn back to the buffet and snort at Lucy. "Poetic."

"I thought so."

We giggle, and head over to join Miranda and her parents.

Chapter Twenty-One

The driver arrives for me at ten-thirty, and most people are heading home at around the same time. I say my goodbyes to everyone in the lobby, including Tom, and hug Miranda and Lucy – they're staying to enjoy the spa facilities and another night at the hotel before jetting off to the Caribbean for two weeks, the lucky sods.

I climb awkwardly into the car and check my phone again as the driver pulls away. I have messages from Jemima and my mum, asking how the wedding went, and I send glowing reports back. There's still no message from Max.

When we arrive back at my building, the driver carries my bags in for me and I spend the rest of the day trying to catch up with a few chores before settling down to read. It's hard to concentrate though because I'm either checking my phone or my mind's wandering to what would have happened with Tom if I'd given in to temptation.

Max finally texts in the evening.

Hi sweetheart, sorry I didn't get back to you sooner. Things have been hectic. How was the wedding? x

It was perfect ☺ Are you still in Germany? x

I'm glad it went well. Yes, heading back tonight. See you on Wed? x

It's a date x

☺ *Goodnight, sweetheart x*

Night xxx

The next two weeks without Lucy are weird and I really miss her. I throw myself into my work, trying to avoid looking over at Tom every ten seconds, and concentrate on giving Max my full attention. My cast is removed, but Tom still insists on giving me lifts to and from work, and I guiltily go along with it.

Unenthusiastically, Mum agrees to another lunch with Max, this time in London, and they head down on the train on the first Saturday of July and meet us in a tapas restaurant. At first, Mum maintains a hurt coolness towards him, but he makes a real effort to engage her on her interests, and she soon starts to thaw out enough to at least be polite back. I've asked Dad to stay away from Australian history or any reference to convicts, and instead he talks at length about the history of alcohol production in an endearing attempt to find common ground with Max.

I sigh with relief when we see them off at the station, and hug Max as I thank him for his effort. It wasn't the most relaxed of meals but at least everyone managed not to offend anyone this time, and I'll take that as a success after the disaster of the first attempt.

We're up to preparing stage three of our ad campaign for

Wild Spirit, and Max comes into the office again to see our progress, then takes me out for a meal after.

"You know it's unusual that you don't just let your marketing department liaise with us, don't you?" I ask him over a plate of sushi.

"I wanted to be in control of choosing our new ad agency," he shrugs.

"Yes, fine, I can see that you'd want to be in charge of the initial selection, but what about afterwards – the day-to-day stuff like coming in to the office today? Don't you think that's a bit OTT for the boss? Shouldn't you be delegating more?"

He shifts uncomfortably in his seat. "I would – usually."

"Why is it different this time?"

"Because of you."

"Oh!" I digest this for a minute, then a pleased smile creeps over my face.

"What are you looking so smug about, madam?" he smirks.

"Just how I've got you wrapped around my little finger, boss," I grin slyly.

"You have as well, you cheeky thing." He tweaks my hair and we smile at each other. It's the first time we've joked like this since he first met my parents and it feels good to get back to normal. He leans in and kisses me softly, and then holds my hand while we finish eating.

Lucy returns from her holiday, all tanned and glowing with happiness. We squeal when we see each other across the office and she comes running over to my desk for a hug. A few people gather round as she gushes about her two-week stay in 'paradise' and we all sigh in envy.

At lunchtime, we go to our favourite café with Tim and she presents us with souvenirs – a dolphin keyring for Tim and a fridge magnet depicting a beautiful piece of Caribbean art for me. While we eat, we catch her up on the latest gossip (there's a rumour that Mike and Evie have been on a date, which Tim is *very* smug about, having predicted it at the Christmas party; and there's another rumour that Tom is being head-hunted by a larger firm, which I try not to think about too much). Lucy greets the news of Mike and Evie with a 'Well, then, there's hope for Stan and Llewellyn yet!', and the rumour about Tom with a sharp but concerned glance at me. I smile reassuringly, but she looks at me doubtfully. Fortunately, Tim changes the subject – he wants us to go out with him and Gemma and bring Miranda and Max, so we arrange a tentative date to confirm with our partners. It's only as we're making our way back to the office that I realise that I haven't arranged for a get-together between Max and my friends before now, not counting the wedding, and I wonder why it hasn't occurred to me.

During the afternoon, Tom stops by my desk to look over some storyboards that I've been working on. He spots the magnet which I'd left out on the top and picks it up.

"It's from Lucy," I tell him.

"It's beautiful – another one for your collection." We smile at each other, then get to work.

After a few minutes, I decide to tentatively ask him about the rumour that he's being head-hunted.

"It's true," he acknowledges humbly.

"Have you made a decision?"

"Not yet."

"Are you leaning more one way than the other?"

"I keep swinging backwards and forwards, to be honest. On the one hand, there's the lure of the bigger firm, and more pay, but on the other hand I haven't even been here a year yet and there's still a lot I want to achieve."

"So, it's fifty-fifty?"

He hesitates. "Not really – there's something else keeping me here." And he looks at me with those sleepy eyes and I flush and look away.

Simon joins us then, and we get back to discussing the storyboards. I try to imagine what it would be like if Tom left – would it be better, because I wouldn't have to see him every day, or worse? I still haven't made my mind up when I lie in bed, tossing and turning for half the night.

On Friday night, Max and I meet up with Lucy, Miranda, Tim and Gemma at an Italian restaurant not far from Tim's place. I get to know Gemma more over garlicky mushroom pasta and rocket and tomato salad and, of course, a few bottles of wine. The more I get to know her, the more I like her. She's down-to-earth and sweet and fits Tim to a tee. I can tell that Lucy approves of her too. In fact, by the end of the meal I realise that I've been concentrating so much on getting to know Gemma that I've barely spoken to Max, who's been talking to Miranda for most of the evening. She's a research scientist, and she's explaining her work to him when I tune in to their conversation after guiltily becoming aware that I've been neglecting him. I'm reminded of their bio-chemist sperm donor, and, when there's a natural pause, I ask when they're planning to go ahead with the insemination.

"Next month," Miranda answers with an excited gleam in her eye, and Lucy smiles and reaches over and clasps her hand.

"How exciting!" Gemma exclaims. "I love babies – that's why I went into neo-natal nursing."

Max grimaces and I look at him in surprise but he doesn't notice, and Lucy starts telling Gemma about the donor they've selected. She moves on to asking her questions about pregnancy and labour, and I soon notice that everyone's contributing to the conversation except for Max. I lean over to him and ask if he's okay.

"Fine – it's just not my idea of dinner conversation," he murmurs back, taking a sip of his water.

I don't know what to say to that – we're with friends, not at a business meeting, so I don't see the problem, but I remind myself that they're *my* friends, not his, and he might not feel as comfortable as I do discussing the personal details of their lives. Gemma seems okay with it though, but she's a woman, and a nurse, so I suppose it's completely different. I place my hand in his, and he smiles at me. The conversation carries on flowing around us.

We finish our meals, and Lucy's all up for going to a club, but I can tell Max doesn't fancy it, so we wave them all off and head back to his house. For the first time, our love-making seems perfunctory, but I remind myself that this is what happens when you've been with someone for a while, and we still fall asleep afterwards in each other's arms.

Max's birthday looms at the end of July, and I rack my brain to think of what to get him. What do you buy a millionaire, for Christ's sake? In the end, I decide on an experience day and book a hot air balloon ride, managing to secure a date on the weekend after his birthday due to a cancellation. I tell him to save the date, and he promises he will.

His birthday falls on a Thursday, and I cook him a meal at my flat. I go for a Moroccan-themed menu, and the flat smells heavenly by the time he arrives from a late business meeting. He looks tired, so I take his coat and pour him a drink and let him relax on the sofa listening to a romantic playlist I made especially for tonight while I do a few last-minute jobs in the kitchen.

Whitesnake is singing *Is This Love?* when the music stops abruptly five minutes after Max has arrived. I head back through to the lounge to check what's happened and Max tells me he's turned it off because he has a headache. I sympathise and offer him some paracetamol, but he's already taken some.

I start serving the food – a selection which includes a mixture of spicy and non-spicy dishes and flatbreads with dips – and we start eating in silence.

"How was your meeting?" I ask at last.

"Stressful," he grunts. "I don't know why people can't just

do their jobs properly."

I put my hand over his in sympathy, and he smiles tiredly at me. "Would you like a massage after we've eaten? It might relax you."

He looks tempted but shakes his head. "To be honest, I think I'll just head home after this. I'm pretty bushed."

I nod in understanding. He eats a little more, then wipes his mouth and puts his napkin down.

"Aren't you having any more?" I ask in surprise.

"No – I had a big meal at lunch time. It was very tasty, though. Thank you." He leans over and kisses me.

"You're welcome," I murmur, a little disappointed. Guess I'll be eating leftovers for a few days, reader.

We relax on the sofa for a bit, my feet in his lap, but I can see that he's flagging and he soon decides it's time for him to head home. I fetch his coat and walk down the stairs with him where he gives me a quick peck on the lips and then he's gone. I make my way back up to the flat to start clearing the table, trying not to feel too downcast that the evening didn't go quite as I'd expected it to.

Saturday dawns bright and beautiful, and Max is in a more cheerful mood when he picks me up at nine. I program the postcode of the launch site into the satnav and say, "Off you go, Miles" to him with a cheeky grin, and he rolls his eyes but smiles and pulls away from the kerb.

We chat about how the rest of our week has been on the journey and I'm pleased that he seems to be feeling a lot more relaxed. When we arrive and he sees what's in store for us, he has an excited gleam in his eye and I'm relieved to hear that hot air ballooning is one of the few adventures he hasn't had. We head inside and register at the desk before having a briefing from our pilot, who's called Richard, and we jump at the opportunity to help inflate the colourful balloon. A burner system is attached to the basket and then the balloon envelope is laid out on the ground. We work well as a team and my breath catches at the look of exuberance on Max's handsome face as the balloon starts filling with air and eventually lifts off the ground.

We board the basket, and the ground crew releases the balloon; the pilot fires a flame from the burner, and we start lifting into the air. I squeal and hold Max's hand as we ascend, and he grins and pulls me in so he can put his arm around me. We watch the landscape get smaller as we rise higher, and we soon have a spectacular view of the surrounding countryside. I feel the air grow cooler, and the houses, cars and trees begin to look like toys dotted around the green landscape.

We're handed champagne flutes, and we drink as we float over the world below. My face starts to ache I'm smiling so much, and Max's blue eyes shine as he takes in the scene beneath us.

"Happy?" I ask him.

"Happy," he murmurs, and I'm reminded of the time he asked me the same thing in our hotel room in Paris, and the memory makes me smile. I think he's remembering too, because he leans in to kiss me, his eyes growing heated.

We stay up for about an hour before it's time to descend, and before I know it we're bumping along the ground at the landing site and being helped out of the basket. We have great fun assisting the crew to deflate the balloon by pushing all the air out and gathering it up to be packed into its stuff sack; it's like packing away a gigantic sleeping bag.

Exhilarated, we return to base and say goodbye to the staff, then walk back to the car hand-in-hand. Once we're inside, he thanks me and kisses me, and we head to a country pub for lunch.

Chapter Twenty-Two

August passes without incident. I see Max regularly, and we have lunch with my mum and dad again and even once with my friends – and although he doesn't really click with them, everyone's polite and friendly and the get-togethers go smoothly. Lucy has her first attempt at artificial insemination, but it doesn't work and she's devastated – I take a bottle of gin around to hers when she finds out and the three of us get pissed and spend the evening ranting about periods and soon feel a lot better. "There's always next month," I remind her, and she hiccups and smiles. Tim buys Gemma his first gift (a record, this far into a relationship), and she's delighted with it. And the rumours about Mike and Evie are confirmed when they start dating openly (opposites attract – who'd have thought it?).

I ask Tom again if he's made a decision about changing firms. He nods.

"And?" I feel butterflies in my tummy as I anxiously await his response. You may be thinking, reader, that I shouldn't be feeling this way about a man who isn't my boyfriend, and you'd be right, but I can't help it. It's not a case of wanting my cake and eating it, or enjoying having someone waiting in the wings (in fact, the whole situation is pretty heart-breaking when I think about it too much), it's just that I like them both – like, *really* like them both – who wouldn't? If only he'd been single when I was … but then I wouldn't have got together with Max, would I?

"And … I've decided to stay," he answers, and I let out the breath I hadn't realised I'd been holding.

"Good," I say with relief.

He cocks an eyebrow. "Not for my heart," he responds wryly, and I grimace.

"I'm sorry," I say with more than a smidgen of guilt.

"It's okay, it's actually a blessing *and* a curse to get to see you every day," he answers matter-of-factly, and in a weird way it's one of the nicest things that anyone's ever said to me. "I don't know what you see in that good-looking millionaire anyway," he adds with his tongue in his cheek, and I guffaw and swat him on the arm. He fakes injury and I roll my eyes. "Does he like twenty-seven and fifty-three?" he asks curiously, after a pause.

"He doesn't like takeaways."

He looks at me in mock horror and shakes his head.

"What about nachos?" he asks with hooded eyes, and I bite my lip and look up at him from under my eyelashes.

We're interrupted by Stan, and I back away and murmur 'See you' then I head back to my desk. I stop and turn when I hear Tom shout my name, though.

"What about fridge magnets?" he calls across the open plan office, and a few people look up from their desks curiously.

I shake my head. "I don't think he's noticed them." And I turn and carry on back to my desk.

It's like the weather knows when September begins; it becomes markedly cooler and by the time we're half-way through the month I notice some of the leaves are already changing colour. I've started babysitting for Jemima and Gideon once a month, and as I haven't seen Max for over a week because he's been in New York, I finally persuade him to come with me.

"It'll be fine," I tell him. "The kids'll be in bed when we get there and the baby doesn't even wake up for a bottle anymore." And he actually reluctantly agrees.

We turn up at their flat to find Jemima looking a million bucks and Gideon's scrubbed up pretty well too. I introduce them to Max and then tell her she looks great. She beams.

"I've lost the baby weight, and feel *so* much better now the children are sleeping through," she answers happily.

"Good for you! I told you that phase wouldn't last forever."

She takes my hand. "You did. It's just hard to put things into perspective when you're going through it."

"Things *always* get better." I gesture between myself and Max, and she nods in understanding and hugs me.

"I'm so pleased for you," she murmurs in my ear, then whispers, "P.S. He's an absolute dish!"

I laugh and Max looks over at us curiously, but I just shake my head at him.

Jemima and Gideon leave so that they'll make it to the theatre on time, and we go and get settled in their living room. I've brought a couple of board games, and Max's eyes light up when I take them out of the bag. He claps his hands together and rubs them in anticipation, and that competitive gleam enters his eyes.

"I hope you're ready to be thrashed, madam."

"Bring it on!" I tell him, and we start setting up the pieces.

Of course, Max wins, and just as I'm demanding a re-match, we hear the baby start to cry. I jump up in surprise and hurry through to the baby's room to find him covered in vomit.

"Oh, you poor thing!" I murmur, and quickly strip off his soiled things so I can cuddle him. Max comes into the room and wrinkles his nose. I find a clean muslin cloth and drape it over my shoulder just as the baby coughs and throws up again. Max jumps back, horrified, and I almost laugh at the look of panic on his face. I rub the baby's back. "There, there, it's okay – let it out and you'll soon feel better." I wipe the baby down as best as I can and ask Max to get me a new muslin. He looks confused and I point to the correct drawer. He manages to find it and then I send him to the bathroom to look for a thermometer. After rummaging around for it for a while, he comes back, holding it up like a prize. Trying not to smile, I take the baby's temperature and it's normal. He hasn't vomited for a while so I decide to give him a bath. I ask Max to change the bedding, and he again looks at me in bemusement. I point to the cupboard where I think the sheets are kept and leave him to work out the rest for himself.

The baby is calm in the bath and I squeak the ducks at him and he giggles. I take him out after ten minutes and wrap him in a towel and start drying him, and that's when Jemima and Gideon's two-year-old, Sophie, starts crying. I call through to Max for him to check on her while I quickly finish drying the baby and start putting on his nappy and a new sleepsuit.

After a minute, Max shoots into the bathroom looking panic-stricken and holding up vomit-covered hands. I point to the sink. Once he's washed them, I hand him the baby and he holds him with his arms out-stretched in front of him. The baby dangles there; he takes one look at Max and starts screaming.

I hurry in to Sophie to find that she is also covered in sick and crying her eyes out.

"Don't worry, sweetheart. Everything's okay. It's just a bit of sick," I tell her as I pull the soiled covers off her and lift her into my arms, grabbing the clean bottom sheet to drape over my shoulder. I rub her back and she starts to calm down. I can still hear the baby screaming, though. I take Sophie through to the baby's room to get the thermometer, then head back to the bathroom. I run her a fresh bath and pop her in, then keep half an eye on her while I turn to take little Harry off Max. He hands him over in relief and the baby stops crying almost instantly. I juggle him and taking Sophie's temperature – also normal – then send Max to change her bedding.

He comes back after a few minutes and I leave him with explicit instructions not to take his eyes off Sophie while I go and try to settle the yawning baby back into his cot. I decide I'll check in on them both regularly for the rest of the evening once they've both gone back to sleep.

The baby goes down easily. I stay stroking his head for a while to make sure he's settled, then hurry back to the bathroom. Max is standing exactly where I left him staring at Sophie. I'm not sure he's even blinked.

"It's okay, I can take over now," I inform him lightly, and he exits the room like a shot.

I take Sophie out of the bath and dry her, putting her in fresh pyjamas, then try to settle her back into bed. However, unlike the baby, she's having none of it. She starts crying as soon as I try to lie her down and clings around my neck like a limpet. I try sitting her on my lap and reading her a book, but as soon as I finish and try to lie her back down, she starts crying again. Eventually, I give up and carry her through to the living room.

"Why have you brought her in here?" he asks, appalled, when we enter the lounge.

"She won't settle."

"What are we going to do with her?"

"Cuddles, stories – hopefully she'll get sleepy soon and nod off." I reach for a box of books and pull one out at random. It's about a rabbit who can't find his mummy.

"How do you know what to do?" Max asks in wonder.

"I babysat for local families when I was a teenager to earn a bit of money."

"You're a natural."

"Thanks," I smile, and start reading the story to Sophie.

I get through four books before her eyes start drooping. I

hold her close as she falls asleep, and when I'm sure she's completely gone, I carry her back upstairs and ease her gently down into the cot bed. She sighs but doesn't wake up, and I tiptoe out of the room. I check on Harry, and he's sleeping peacefully, then I head back to the lounge.

I flop onto the sofa and surprise both myself and Max by bursting into tears.

"Oh my God, what's wrong?" he asks in a panic.

I shake my head and keep crying. He pulls me against him and I soak the front of his shirt with my tears as he strokes my back and makes soothing noises.

Eventually, my sobs subside, and I take a few shuddering breaths.

"Are you going to tell me what that was all about?" he asks once my breathing evens out.

I shake my head against his chest.

"Is it … is it about the baby that you lost?" he asks gently after a pause. I give a small nod and he sighs and kisses the top of my head.

"I-I never g-got chance to look after him when h-he was ill, or bathe him, or-or soothe him to sleep, or r-read to him," I tell him, shivering. I suddenly feel icy cold.

"I know, sweetheart. I'm so sorry," he answers softly, squeezing me tighter.

We sit like that for a while. He rubs my back and I cling to him.

"You haven't said what people usually say to me," I tell

him after a while.

"What's that?" he murmurs.

"That I can always have other children."

"You can."

I look up at him. "With you?" The thought hasn't occurred to me before, but I'm suddenly curious as to his answer.

There's a pause, and then he shakes his head sadly. "I don't want to have any," he admits reluctantly.

"With anyone?"

"With anyone."

"Oh."

I think about this for a while.

"Is that a problem?" he finally asks softly.

I bite my lip. "It might be." And he sighs.

"You've seen what I'm like with kids."

"You could learn."

"I don't want to," he tells me gently.

"Ah."

I cling to him, but I feel a little crack appear in my heart in the place that's reserved for him. He squeezes me as if to stop me from floating away, and it's only the baby crying out that makes us reluctantly pull apart.

I brush my cheeks and stand up and walk away from him. I enter Harry's room to find him still sleeping peacefully. I touch his forehead and it feels fine so I pop into Sophie's room to check on her too. She's curled up on her side, sucking her thumb, sound asleep. I ease back out of the room and tip-toe back to the lounge.

Max opens his arms to me and I fall into them.

"Tell me about your husband," he murmurs.

"Matt? He was a fireman. We met on a night out when I was twenty-one."

"I can't imagine what it's like to lose someone you love in that way."

"Car accidents happen every day. And it was Christmas time – there are always people willing to risk drink-driving at that time of year when they wouldn't at any other time."

"And the other driver's still in prison?"

I nod, and we lapse into silence.

"He was having an affair, you know," I finally tell him in a matter-of-fact voice.

"Matt was?"

"Hmm. I've never told anyone this before. I found out just before Christmas. I was devastated. He swore he would finish it, and I wanted to believe him. I was five months pregnant and terrified of being alone. But just before the crash, I'd discovered a new text from her and we were arguing about it. That's when the lorry hit us." Max squeezes me tight and rests his head on mine. "I was struggling for a while," I continue softly, "and then this man came into my life. He saw potential in me and took me out of my comfort zone. He made me feel things I hadn't felt for a long time, and I'm so, so grateful to him."

"Oh God, that sounds like goodbye," he groans, and a tear

spills onto my cheek.

We're still sitting like that when Jemima and Gideon return. They're a little tipsy and don't notice anything wrong. I smile as she gushes about the show they went to see and grimace when I have to burst her bubble and tell her about the children's sickness.

"Touch wood, they've been fine since, though," I reassure her tiredly. I'm emotionally exhausted, and Max looks wiped out too. Jemima goes to check on them and reports back that they're both sound asleep. She hugs me and thanks me for looking after them, and Max and I start gathering our things to leave.

The drive back to mine is completed in companionable silence. Max holds my hand when he's not changing gear and rubs his thumb across my finger gently. When we get to my building, he walks me to the door.

"Can we stay in touch?" he asks, holding both my hands in his. I bite my lip and nod, and he leans in to kiss me tenderly. "I wish things could be different," he murmurs.

"Me too."

We smile at each other, and I get my key out. He takes it from me and inserts it into the lock, then he's pushing the door open for me and I'm walking through it. I shut it softly behind me.

When I lie in bed that night, I find myself really missing Vanessa's comforting presence, but remind myself that, thanks to Max, I don't need her anymore. I meant what I said when I told him I was grateful. He'll never know what he saved me from.

Chapter Twenty-Three

The rest of September is pretty miserable. More than once I'm tempted to phone Max and beg for us to start over again, but then I remember the reason why we'd never work, and I stop myself. We do text each other a couple of times, and I'm glad we agreed to stay in touch. To be fair to Tom, he tells me he's sorry when he hears the news, and he seems to have decided to give me space to get over the break up because he doesn't try anything. In fact, as time goes on, I begin to wonder if he's even still interested, or if it was just the thrill of the competition. Maybe he's waiting for me to make the first move? Either way, I'm grateful. I'm not ready to rush into anything else yet. My heart needs time to heal again.

The only good news to come out of September is that Lucy gets a positive pregnancy test. I find out mid-morning on the last day of the month when I open my desk draw and find the test in there, with the word PREGNANT clearly written in the little window. I scream and a few people near me jump out of their seats, but I don't care as I rush over to my best friend and hug her so tightly I fear I might break her.

"What took you so long?" she laughs as we jump up and down. "I've been watching you all bloody morning waiting for you to open that flippin' drawer!"

"I'm sorry! Oh God, I'm so frickin' happy for you both!" I say as we stop bouncing around. There are tears pouring down my face.

"This'll be you again one day," she tells me earnestly, wiping her eyes, and I nod.

"Of course it will."

I rush over to Tom's office and stick my head around the door. I give him my best puppy dog eyes.

"What do you want?" he asks in amusement when he looks up from his computer.

"Can Lucy and I take an early lunch break today? I *promise* we'll be back within the hour."

His eyebrows quirk up. "What's the occasion? I heard the screams in here."

I bite my lip. "It's a secret – for now."

He narrows his eyes playfully. "Alright then, but you'll owe me."

I pretend to think about it. "Deal."

I head inside and shake his hand firmly. He holds on and looks at me through lowered lids.

"You don't know what you're agreeing to yet."

"I trust you," I tell him, and he grins a wicked grin. My mouth goes dry.

"Go and enjoy your 'lunch'."

I salute and turn smartly on my heel, and I hear him

chuckle behind me as I make my way out of the office.

Lucy and I head to our usual café, and we're not there five minutes before she's looking over the menu and moaning about all the soft cheeses and patés that she's not allowed to eat now. I roll my eyes.

"You never ate any of those things anyway," I remind her.

"But at least I had the option to if I wanted," she protests.

I shake my head in exasperation and steer the conversation in a new direction. "How did Miranda react to the test?"

"She turned deathly pale and I thought she was going to faint. I had to sit her down on the toilet and get her to put her head between her knees for ten minutes."

"Oh, bless her!"

"I think it suddenly became real to her. She's fine now. She's been texting me all morning asking how I'm feeling and suggesting gender-neutral colour schemes for the nursery."

"How exciting!"

"We're going to wait until the twenty-week scan before we start buying anything though."

"Sensible."

"I've got to be sensible now; I'm going to be a parent."

We look at each other and 'Eek!' at the same time. A couple of other customers turn to look at us curiously but we ignore them.

The waitress comes over and we order our food. We spend the rest of the hour discussing morning sickness and pregnancy pillows, antenatal checks and pain relief options, and before we know it, it's time to head back to the office.

It's been a little over an hour by the time we step out of the lift, and while Lucy heads to the toilet I exaggeratedly tip-toe past Tom's glass-fronted office. He's on the phone, and he smirks and wags his finger at me as he watches me make my way comedically to my desk. I grimace and mouth 'sorry' and he shakes his head in exasperation but smiles.

I'm less miserable in October, though it's hard when Max comes into the office to see how stage four of our ad campaign for Wild Spirit is progressing. He kisses me on the cheek when he enters the conference room, and I inhale his familiar spicy male scent. It brings back lots of memories, and I smile at him wistfully. He winks and we settle into our seats. Tom leads the presentation with Simon's input and when it's finished, Max declares himself satisfied.

He asks me to escort him to the lift, and I see Tom watching as he places his hand on my lower back to guide me out of the room. We walk past reception, and he asks me how I'm doing.

"I'm fine," I tell him. "You know, adjusting. How about you?"

"The same." He sighs. "I miss you."

I reach out and squeeze his hand. "I miss you too."

"I just wish things could be different."

"I know."

The lift arrives, and he kisses my cheek and I let his hand go, then he's stepping in and the doors are sliding shut.

I stand there staring at the doors for a while, then shake myself and turn to find Tom behind me. "Alright?" he asks softly.

I nod, but my lip wobbles. He steps forward and gives me a hug, and I lean into him.

"It's hard, I know," he murmurs against my hair.

"It's just that he was the first man I've … dated since …"

"I know, sweetheart."

I sigh shakily, and pull away. "You haven't told me what I owe you for that early lunch yet," I try to smile at him.

He hesitates. "I was going to leave it a bit longer."

"Oh God, have you got some kind of Red Room of Pain or something?"

He barks a laugh. "Jesus, nothing like that!"

"What then?" I ask curiously.

"Well … I was going to invite you out to the fireworks display at the park for bonfire night."

"Oh. Well, that sounds pain-free."

"Are you … up for something like that yet?"

I bite my lip. "Yes, I think so."

His eyes light up. "Great!"

We head back past reception, and Tom goes into his office whistling.

The next week, I'm working quietly at my desk when Jean calls me to ask me to come to reception. Surprised, I make my way over to discover Jemima, Sophie and Harry waiting for me. All three are crying, the children deafeningly, and Jemima's face is a mess of mascara.

"I'm so sorry – I didn't know where else to go," she sobs as I reach her side and take Harry from her.

"What's happened? Is it Gideon? Has something happened to him?" I ask, my heart racing.

"No, no – he's fine; he's away for work. I just – Harry hasn't been sleeping again. I think he's having some sort of sleep regression or something. The books say he's due one at this age. Or maybe it's teething, I don't know," she babbles, as more tears flood down her face, which now I'm closer, I can see shows all the signs of one very exhausted mummy. "He's been crying all morning, and Sophie has been tantrumming – it's the terrible twos, you know. I thought I'd get us all out of the house, but they're just as bad as they were *in* the house, and – and – I was getting to my wit's end and I saw your office building, and –" She bursts into a new flood of tears and the cries of the children get even louder. I hug her with my free arm.

"Here, give her to me," Tom's voice says from behind me, and he reaches for Sophie and lifts her expertly into his arms. "Jean, can you hunt out some crayons and paper for me, please?" he calls over to reception. Jemima looks at him gratefully as he passes her a tissue. I introduce them over the noise of the children's wailing.

"This is Tom. Tom, this is Jemima."

"Thank you, Tom," she tells him and he nods and looks carefully at Harry.

"Have you tried any infant paracetamol?"

"I was going to pick some up while I was out," she answers, her breath hitching.

"His cheeks are very red – you might be right about the teething."

"He's always sailed through new eruptions before."

"From experience of my sister's kids, it can be different each time," he tells her.

Lisa arrives to see what's going on, and Tom hands her his wallet and asks her to go to the local chemist to buy the medicine. Not long after, Jean returns with the paper and crayons, and Tom takes them from her and sets them on the low table in front of the sofa. He crouches down and puts Sophie next to him and starts drawing without saying anything to her. She starts to quieten down as she watches curiously. He sketches rapidly and a rabbit soon emerges on the page. Sophie points to it and says 'bunny rabbit' and Tom points to another piece of paper and puts a crayon on top for her. Shyly, she picks it up and starts making marks. He encourages her gently, and she's soon smiling and scribbling with abandon.

Jemima looks on in relief, and smiles gratefully when Jean returns with coffee. She drinks it while I walk back and forth with Harry.

When Lisa returns, she brings teething gel as well as the paracetamol. I tell her she's a diamond and she glows. I hold Harry for Jemima as she administers the correct dose of the medicine and smears the gel on his sore gums. All this time, Tom is chatting quietly to Sophie, making her giggle by deliberately misnaming the animals that he draws for her to colour in.

Before long, Harry's cries turn to whimpers, and he soon starts yawning. I settle him into his pushchair and start rocking it back and forth slowly. He's asleep within five minutes.

I continue for a few more minutes then gradually slow down before bringing the pushchair to a stop. Harry doesn't stir. Jean brings more coffee for us all and I sit down beside Jemima and put my arm around her as we take sips. We talk softly. I tell her what a great job she's doing, and that this is just another phase to get through before things get better again; that parenting is bloody hard and how much I admire her. I tentatively ask if she's still taking her medication and she confirms that she is with a nod. I tell her that's good – that sometimes we need a little help to get through life's difficult times.

"I was once in a low place, and needed help like that," I tell her softly. "My mind made up its own coping strategies, and it took time to return to some semblance of normality … but I got there. And you will too." She sniffs back tears as I talk, and hugs me tightly when I finish. Tom catches my eye over her shoulder, and winks supportively.

Jemima stays for over an hour after that, drinking coffee and chatting with me quietly while Harry continues to sleep and Tom occupies Sophie with the drawing materials. Lisa brings some biscuits over to us and I thank her warmly. Eventually, Jemima tells us that she'd better be heading home.

"Do you want me to come with you?" I ask, looking at Tom, who nods at my unvoiced request to leave early.

"No, no – I'll be fine," she answers.

"Are you sure? What about if I come round after work to help you out and keep you company?"

"That would be great. Gideon's not back until tomorrow," she smiles gratefully, and Tom says he'll drop me at their house straight from work. He asks Sophie if she'd like to keep the crayons and pictures and she beams and clutches them tightly to her chest.

I see the three of them into the lift and wave goodbye as the doors slide shut.

"Thank you so much for being so understanding and helpful," I say to Tom when I turn around and find him still there. He waves away my gratitude.

"I only did what I'd want someone to do for my sister."

"Still – you were wonderful."

"She's lucky to have such a good friend."

"She'd do the same for me."

"Kids are hard work, especially when you've got two little ones like that."

"Did you … did you and Melanie ever discuss having any?" I ask tentatively.

"Yes, but it was always in some distant future. I never really even pictured what it would be like, to be honest. At least, not with her …"

I flush at the look in his eyes, but I'm saved from responding by Lisa arriving to tell him there's a phone call waiting for him.

Chapter Twenty-Four

Tom steps up the flirting over the next few weeks, and I can't deny that I thoroughly enjoy it. He often calls me into the office on some pretext of going over the progress of one of our campaigns with me, but it's really a chance for him to tease me.

He does it for the third time in one day just over a week after Jemima's visit and I enter his office and stand in front of his desk with my hand on my hips. He leans back in his chair, his hands clasped across his flat stomach, and his eyes travel up and down my body seductively. I'm wearing a shortish pencil skirt and a grey tank top with a white blouse underneath. I suddenly realise how much like a school girl I must look.

I smirk and cock my eyebrow. "You know, I could make a complaint of sexual harassment about this," I tell him archly, but of course, secretly I'm loving it.

"Why don't you then?" he asks lazily.

"Because that would spoil all the fun."

"Speaking of fun – could you just fetch me the top file from the bottom drawer over there." He points to a filing cabinet which is against the wall opposite to his desk, and I know exactly what he wants.

I roll my eyes but make my way over, swaying my hips in what I hope is a sexy way and trying desperately not to trip over my own feet. When I reach the filing cabinet, I bend over to reach the bottom drawer, keeping my legs straight, and take my time retrieving the file, then I straighten up and slowly make my way back over to him, biting my lip the whole time. He watches with hooded eyes. I slap the file on top of his desk and place my hands to either side of it. The top three buttons of my blouse are undone and the neckline gapes as I lean forwards. His eyes flick down and I smirk.

"Is there anything else I can do for you, *sir*?" I ask sweetly, and his eyes blaze.

"Well now, there's a question with a lot of potential," he murmurs. We stare into each other's eyes, and electricity seems to crackle between us. I feel heat flooding my body and I nearly throw myself across the desk at him, glass wall or no, but we're interrupted by Llewellyn's knock at the door.

"Come in!" Tom barks without taking his eyes off me. I straighten up and try to look away, but I can't.

"Erm – am I interrupting something?" Llewellyn asks hesitantly.

"Not at all," I tell him lightly, but I still don't look away from Tom, who has a wicked gleam in his eyes.

After an awkward pause, Llewellyn clears his throat. I decide to bring this interesting interlude to an end.

"Will that be all, *sir*?"

"For now, thank you. You've been most helpful."

"Any time." And I pivot and sway out of the room, winking at Llewellyn as I pass him, and he chuckles.

Before I know it, November arrives, and with it the promise of my payment to Tom for that early lunch. I dress appropriately for the night ahead, wrapping myself up in several layers including a hoodie and my warmest coat, together with tights, jeans and boots. As I'm donning my hat and scarf, I catch sight of one of the motivational posters I have dotted around my flat. I look around at the others and realise how far I've come in nearly a year, and give myself a pat on the back for a job well done before I finally put my gloves on and go switching off most of the lights and head out into the cold night to meet Tom at the entrance to the park.

He's already there when I arrive, looking ruddy-cheeked and broad-shouldered in his thick winter coat, his breath fogging in the icy air like mine. His eyes light up when he sees me, and he kisses me on the cheek and takes my hand to lead me inside. He pays the entrance fee, and then we make our way through the crowd.

"Rides first or hot chocolate by the fire?" he asks, and I opt for the rides.

We go on several, chatting and laughing while we queue up for each, and yelling and giggling when we're spinning on the Waltzers and chasing each other in the bumper cars.

I feel breathless with exhilaration when we get off the fifth ride, and we decide to have a break. Tom purchases hot chocolates and burgers, and we go and stand by the huge bonfire. We lean against the protective railing, feeling the heat of the fire warm the front of our bodies while our backs remain cold against the night. The light from the fire dances over Tom's face, highlighting the planes and angles of his stubbled jaw and cheekbones, and I catch my breath at his masculine beauty.

"Having fun?" he asks softly, as he catches me looking at him. I nod. He hesitates, and then leans in to kiss me gently on the lips before pulling back. I smile at him shyly and he squeezes my hand. "You look even more beautiful in firelight, if that's even possible." And I tell him I was thinking the same about him.

We finish our drinks and head back to the rides. He takes me on the ghost train, which is so bad it's funny, and the Ferris wheel, where we sit close and admire the view of the distant lights of the city twinkling in the darkness.

Before we know it, it's time for the fireworks display, and we join the rest of the crowd *oohing* and *aahing* as the bright colours streak and explode against the night sky. The air comes alive with bangs and whizzes, and a layer of thin smoke soon sits above the ground. Tom puts his arm around my shoulder as we watch the spectacle, and I lean against him comfortably.

We stay until the end, and then make our way slowly out of the park with the flow of the crowd. Tom walks me home, and we soon leave everyone behind as we turn the few streets to arrive on my road. Our gloved hands are clasped, and he strokes his thumb over my fingers as we stroll without talking.

We arrive at my building and we stop and stare at each other, then he pulls me into him and wraps his arms around me. He dips his head and gives me what I feel like I've been waiting for forever. His lips move over mine, at first gently, but then with increasing hunger, and soon he's pushing me back against the door and we're breathing hard and clutching at each other desperately.

"Fuck!" he breathes as we come up for air.

"Yes, please," I murmur without thinking, and bite my lip as his eyes blaze. I take out my key and open the door, then walk inside and up the stairs without looking back. I hear him following behind me.

I get to the entrance of my bedroom, and stop. He comes up behind me and presses against my back. His hands start rubbing up and down my arms and shoulders slowly. I lean against him and tilt my head to the side, and he starts kissing my neck. Electricity shoots down my spine and liquid heat pools between my legs. I turn and wrap my arms around his neck, and then his lips are once again on mine.

"My, what soft lips you have, sir," I break away to murmur.

"*All the better to kiss you with, my dear,*" he growls, and he does just that. *Very* thoroughly.

He walks me backwards and we start yanking off each other's clothes. The backs of my legs eventually bump into my bed and I go toppling backwards. He follows me down, bracing himself above me as we continue to kiss hungrily. More clothes get pulled off, and I run my hands over his muscled arms and chest then up around his neck again. I'm panting with want. He starts working his way down my body, but I pull him back up by tugging on his hair.

"*Now*," I urge, and he doesn't need telling twice. He slides into me easily, and we start moving in rhythm immediately. If this was a year ago, the Kings of Leon would be belting out *Sex on Fire* right about now. I scratch my nails gently down his back, and he shudders.

"*God*, you're amazing," he groans, and I look up into his face to see him gazing down at me with so much passion in his eyes that my breath hitches. I cup his face, and he kisses me. We continue on in this way, and I discover that he's a talker. I won't repeat everything that he says, but *damn*, it's hot and he leaves me feeling like the most desirable woman in the world. Before I know it, I feel that beautiful pressure building (you know the one I mean, reader), and I'm crying out in ecstasy just before he does. We lie panting and shuddering in each other's arms, until our breathing returns to normal.

We lie stroking each other softly for hours after that, murmuring about anything and everything. He tells me about the future he wants us to have and I smile and tell him, "Great minds think alike," which makes him chuckle quietly.

Eventually we start yawning. Just before I drift off to sleep, I murmur, "Thanks for waiting for me," and he kisses me tenderly, and I snuggle into his arms.

I wake up the next morning to breakfast in bed. Tom brings it on a tray. It's an omelette, and I smile as I remember the last time he cooked me one. We tease each other gently as we eat, and at one point I arch my eye and tell him I thought he'd be a spanker. He barks a laugh.

"I only do that when little minxes steal the last of the nachos."

"That's a pity," I answer, looking at him from beneath my eyelashes, and he growls and takes the tray off me before pouncing on me and kissing my breath away. I laugh as he rolls me over then yelp as he swats me on the behind.

"Is that what you wanted, madam?"

"I think I prefer the kisses, sir."

"Then that's what you'll have, madam." And he turns me back over and I'm soon panting beneath him.

The morning's passed by the time we get up and shower. While I'm taking my turn, Tom pops to the shop for the Sunday papers and we spend the afternoon reading them and snacking. I smile secretly as I watch him nibbling the chocolate off the outside of a Kit Kat.

As the evening starts, he reluctantly declares that it's time to head home. I escort him downstairs and we kiss goodbye lingeringly, and then he's gone and I'm heading back upstairs. However, just as I get to the top, I hear a knock at the door. I go back down and open it and Tom grabs me and starts kissing me passionately. When he breaks off, I laugh and push him back out the door, and he salutes and jogs away. I head back up to the flat smiling.

The next few weeks pass in a blur. Tom stops over at mine most nights and I start staying at his place sometimes. At work, he still teases me mercilessly in private but we go out of our way to act professionally when in public. The first chance I get to tell Lucy that Tom and I are an item, she shouts, "Yesss!" in the café and, as usual, we get a few looks, which, also as usual, we ignore.

"I just *knew* you were meant to be," she gushes, with tears in her eyes, reaching out to clasp my hand on the table. "As soon as I saw you dancing together at the wedding when you were still wearing that bloody cast."

"But I was with Max then."

"He was what you needed as a stepping stone to get you out there again. Tom's the one you're supposed to be with," she tells me confidently.

"I'm not sure Max would take being called a 'stepping stone' that well," I say drily.

She waves this away then bites her lip. "I wasn't going to tell you this, but now the circumstances have changed ..."

"Tell me what?"

"Miranda saw Max out one night recently ... he was on a date." She looks at me worriedly.

I think about this for a moment and decide I'm happy for him. I'll always think of him as the man who saved me from myself, and remember our time fondly, but Lucy's right – Tom's the one I'm supposed to be with. Max and I wouldn't have worked. Babies are a deal-breaker for me. I tell her so, and she sighs with relief.

"So ... how was it?" she asks eventually, with a sly look in her eyes, and I know exactly what she's talking about.

I take a breath. "It was – *wow!*" I tell her, my cheeks

flushing as I remember the passion of that first night, and that shit-eating grin of hers spreads across her face. Satisfied, she moves on to talk of her morning sickness, which is getting better, and her excitement about the twelve-week scan, which is at the end of December.

I tell her what it's like to have the cold jelly smeared on your tummy and the ultrasound scanner pressed into your abdomen as the sonographer manoeuvres to find the best spot to 'see' the baby, and then the unforgettable feeling as you see your baby's image for the first time. We smile through tears at each other, and she says, "You never would have spoken about this a year ago. You've come so far. I'm bloody proud of you, mate." And I nod in acknowledgement, and it's soon time to go back to work.

I tell Mum and Dad by greeting them at the station hand-in-hand with Tom one Sunday when they come down for a visit. Mum gasps and clasps her hands together before hugging him tightly, and Dad winks at me and shakes Tom's hand and pats him on the back.

"I knew it!" Mum declares. "On your birthday, I just knew it!" And I roll my eyes at Tom but he just smiles.

We walk to the pub where we're having Sunday lunch and Mum reminds Tom of his Tarot card reading, which turned out to be an eery premonition. However, she soon changes the subject to her new hobby, which is candle making. Apparently, the kitchen is full of pots and pans, different types of waxes, wicks, thermometers and other specialist paraphernalia, and the living room is already looking like a church on a holy day. Dad gives us a history lesson on the use of candles throughout the ages, and Tom once again demonstrates that he's spent *way* too much time watching *The History Channel*. The meal passes pleasantly, and Mum hatches an idea to invite Tom and his parents to Christmas dinner. I start to protest – I haven't even met them properly myself yet and it's still fairly early days with Tom, though we're practically living together already – but to my surprise Tom tells her he thinks it's a great idea.

"What about your sister's family?" I ask in concern.

"They usually spend Christmas Day with her husband's family, then come to our parents' place on Boxing Day."

"Oh."

"That's settled then," says Mum smugly. "I'll call Anne tonight."

November passes into December. Jean decorates reception with a little Christmas tree and a cheery garland, and I smile at it when I pass every day on my way to my desk, which is now mine permanently. Tom begs me not to offer 'Pounds for Kisses' this year because he swears it will bankrupt him.

On the day before the office Christmas party, Max comes for his last meeting. He's decided to pass responsibility on to his marketing department, and I think that's for the best. He tells me he's met someone new – a career woman who doesn't want any children – and that they're taking it slowly. I tell him how pleased I am for him and admit softly that I've started seeing Tom. He takes my hand and tells me he's happy for me, then shakes Tom's hand when he joins us.

"I had an inkling," he tells him drily, and Tom smirks.

The ad series for the Wild Spirit brand is at the point when the couple finally get together in full Christmas colour. We sit and watch it in the dimmed conference room, and when the lights go up, I have to brush away a tear from seeing my vision come to completion.

"Well done," Max leans across to murmur to me, and Tom winks at me. Then Max says more loudly, "It's really excellent, everyone. Great work, thank you."

He shakes everyone's hand as they leave the room, then, when only Tom and I are left, he says thoughtfully, "You know, I'm not sure that has to be the end of the story."

I frown. "Oh?"

"Well, what happens to them next?"

I open my mouth to give an answer then snap it shut as I realise that I don't have one.

Tom puts his arm around my shoulder. "Leave it with us," he tells him, and Max nods and smiles.

I escort him to the lift, and peck him on the cheek before he steps inside, and then he's gone.

Chapter Twenty-Five

It's the night of the office Christmas party. I smooth the *Berry Blush* gloss over my lips and make a popping sound as I rub them together. The livid red stays in place perfectly and I twirl in front of my reflection while Nina Simone sings *Feeling Good* on the radio. My phone dings to tell me that the cab has arrived, and I hurry around turning most of the lights off in my little flat, which I spend so little time in these days.

I rush down the stairs, taking care not to twist my ankle, and pull open the door. Then I'm tottering through the dark and clambering into the cab, where I greet Tom with a kiss. I don't notice a single thing about the driver as the twenty-minute journey passes.

Tom has informed the HR department about our relationship, and although we're not planning to flaunt it, we're more relaxed about being seen to be dating openly.

We arrive at our destination where Tom pays the driver and we get out. He wraps his arm around me and we head towards the bar where the smokers are already gathered outside getting their first hit of nicotine of the evening, the vapours dissipating up into the air.

We enter the warm interior and look around for Tim and Lucy before spotting them in a booth. They greet us cheerfully as we arrive at the table and get settled. It's a 'no partners' night but the four of us went out with Miranda and Gemma only last weekend and we ended up in a club, dancing until the wee hours. I had far too many G&Ts and Tom had to carry me out in a fireman's lift to get me into the cab. I had a killer headache the next day.

Lucy and Tim's glasses are nearly empty, so Tom decides to head to the bar. "Is it a free bar tonight?" I murmur to him before he leaves the table.

"Until ten," he smirks. "How are you getting on with those contact lenses now?"

I swat his arm, and he walks off laughing. To make it clear, reader, I have twenty-twenty vision.

"So, who's going to get off with whom this year?" Lucy asks as Whitney Houston's *I'm Your Baby Tonight* plays over the sound-system.

"Me and Tom," I wink.

She rolls her eyes.

"Mike and Evie," Tim grins, and we look over to see them talking to Tom at the bar, hand-in-hand, and smile at each other.

"I'm still plumping for Stan and Llewellyn," Lucy says stubbornly, and Tim and I groan. "What? It could happen one of these years," she insists, and we shake our heads.

"Yeah, the year that you turn straight," Tim declares. Lucy rolls her eyes.

We look over at the side of the dance floor where Stan and Llewellyn are studiously ignoring each other like usual.

"Oh, for Christ's sake!" Lucy bursts out. She jumps up and marches over to them. We stare with our mouths open as she starts pointing at them both belligerently, her face a picture of annoyance and frustration as she tells them what's what.

Tom comes back to the table with a tray of drinks, and frowns.

"What are you – ?"

"Shhh!" We wave at him to be quiet, and I point over at where Stan and Llewellyn are glancing at each other self-consciously as Lucy continues to rant.

"No way," Tom mutters as he takes a seat and joins us in watching the show.

Lucy finishes, and marches back to the table with pursed lips. She grabs the orange juice from the tray and gulps it down in one then wipes her mouth with the back of her hand. Then she notices the expressions on our faces and bursts out laughing.

"I can't believe you just did that," Tim tells her in disbelief.

"Believe it," she answers tartly.

We look back over at Stan and Llewellyn, expecting them to be back to ignoring each other, and we all do a comedy double-take. Stan is tentatively sidling closer to Llewellyn. We hold our breaths as he opens his mouth to say something then closes it.

"Go on," Lucy urges under her breath.

He seems to gather his courage, and then he speaks. I have no idea what he says but Llewellyn looks gobsmacked. They exchange a few words and then Llewellyn puts his hand on his heart and appears to almost melt. Stan takes his hand and speaks earnestly, and Llewellyn starts nodding and wiping at his eyes. They start laughing and talking at once, and then Stan seems to ask a question, and Llewellyn bites his lip and nods. They put down their drinks on a nearby table, and walk out of the bar with their arms linked and their heads close together.

"Holy shit!" Lucy breathes.

I look at her with wide eyes and raise my hand solemnly for a high-five, then we burst into happy laughter.

"I fucking knew it," she declares, and to give her credit, she did.

The rest of the evening goes as you've probably predicted. The CEO gives a speech, followed by a better one from Tom; I drink far too many G&Ts (again) and end up roping Tom into singing with me on the karaoke. We do a pretty good rendition of Sonny and Cher's *I Got You Babe* and then he helps me off the stage, making it two years in row that I don't fall off. Tom finally tips me into a cab at two a.m. and we go back to mine and he helps me take off my clothes and makeup while I sing Tina Turner's *Simply the Best* to him at the top of my voice.

The next day is Sunday, and I have a hangover. I spend the day drinking copious amounts of water and forcing Tom to watch *Pretty Woman* while snuggled under my duvet on the sofa. Mr. Fluffles sits on top of my hip purring, and all's well with the world.

The last week before the Christmas holiday flies by. Instead of 'Kisses for a Pound' for the donkey sanctuary, I do a raffle with prizes I've charmed off local businesses, and make nearly three hundred pounds.

Friday is the last day of work and the office closes at one. At twelve-thirty, I help Jean to give out glasses of champagne and we open our Secret Santa presents. I have been gifted with a gin miniature and a fridge magnet depicting Van Gogh's self-portrait. I suspect Tom twisted a few arms until he found out who'd pulled my name out of the hat and I look over at him where's he's making no attempt to hide his attention, and frown mock-sternly at him. He smirks sexily and winks.

On Saturday, which is the day before Christmas Eve, we drop presents around to Jemima and Gideon and their children. Harry is back to sleeping through the night and Jemima looks like a completely different woman from the day she turned up at the office. We stay for a cuppa and play with the children.

Just before we leave, I sit with Harry on my lap reading him a story. Curious, Sophie gets up from where she's playing with some shapes with Tom as he lounges on the floor, and comes and leans against my leg to look at the pages. I finish the book and she demands another, so I let her choose one, and start reading it, pointing at the pictures and asking questions as I tell the story. At one point, I look up and catch Tom staring at me with such a look of utter devotion on his face that I catch my breath and stumble over the words I was saying. I find my place again and keep reading, but I can feel my heart beating a little faster and my cheeks feel warm.

I finish the story and we say our goodbyes. Tom takes my hand and kisses it as we walk back to the car.

We drive to my mum and dad's in the afternoon of Christmas Eve. We listen to non-stop festive songs on the radio and sing along. I tell him about last year's Christmas dinner and he grimaces at the story of Joy's tactless comments, laughs at Margaret's non-stop references to piles and diarrhoea, growls at Mum's attempt at match-making with Arthur, and puts his hand over mine sympathetically when I describe how the meal ended with Dad having to put me to bed.

"This year will be better," he tells me firmly.

"It already is," I tell him, clasping his hand.

Mum comes running out the door of their house as the car pulls up. "There you are, darling!" she gushes and gives me air kisses on each cheek before doing the same to Tom. She links arms with me and guides me inside as Dad greets Tom and helps him collect our bags from the boot. "I've been absolutely *dying* to show you my candle creations," she continues proudly, and I tell her that I can't *wait* to see them.

We enter the house and they're literally everywhere – on the windowsills, on the mantle, on the coffee table, even going up the stairs. I turn to Dad, who has just come in behind us, and widen my eyes. He chuckles.

"Wow!" I say, and Mum beams. I examine them more

closely, and see that she has a preference for experimenting with the candles' colour and shape – there are blue cylinders, yellow pyramids, pink cuboids and green spirals, to name a few. The whole thing is obviously bizarre, but they're actually quite sweet and she's clearly spent a lot of time perfecting the craft. I can see it makes her happy, so I tell her I'm impressed. She positively glows. Dad winks at me.

As usual, Mum has prepared a buffet for my return as if she's planning on feeding the five thousand. Tom and I stuff ourselves on prawn and mayo sandwiches, sausage rolls and pork pie, then head to unpack our bags. Tom looks amazed as we enter my room, which is still exactly the same as it was last year. He studies the fan-girl posters on the wall and smiles at the yin and yang quilt cover on the bed.

After we've unpacked, we spend some time in the shed with my dad while he does some of his wine-making. Demijohns bubble away, and he teaches Tom how to suck on a tube to transfer the liquid from one container to another. It's relaxing to sit on a rickety old table and watch them pottering away, my dad's pipe in his mouth while AC/DC's *Have a Drink on Me* plays on the old radio. He gives us some samples to try, and we grade them out of ten for their sweetness and body. Mum joins us after a while, and by the end of the session the two of us are more than a little tipsy. She decides to teach us how to make a simple candle, and we go into the house and work in the kitchen, melting wax and pouring it into containers, Mum and I giggling, before finishing off the buffet for tea.

The evening is spent watching *A Christmas Carol*, as usual, and I smile at the reminder that it's never too late for good things to happen.

At 10:30, we kiss each other goodnight and I fall asleep with Tom spooned around me. He's been very attentive today, and I think he's trying to be especially considerate given how hard I find the festive period. We snuggle under the covers, and although the room is slightly too warm, I fall into a deep and dreamless sleep.

Mum wakes us at eight the next morning, excited to see us open our presents, like we're still kids. We humour her and pad downstairs in our pyjamas, greeting my dad, who's likewise been prised out of bed, with a 'Merry Christmas' and a peck on the cheek from me and a hand shake and slap on the back from Tom. Festive music is already playing on the stereo, and our presents are arranged in piles – one for each of us. I smile at the family tradition, pleased to see a pile for Tom has been added, and add my own gifts to my mum and dad's piles as Mum brings bacon sandwiches through from the kitchen.

We eat and open our presents at the same time. Among other gifts, I receive my favourite perfume and a book called *Candle Making for Beginners*. Mum is pleased with her silk scarf and Dad loves his new briefcase. Cheekily, among a few other things, I gifted Tom with a voucher for the Chinese takeaway and he grins when he sees it and kisses me softly on the lips. I open my present from him and discover a necklace with a butterfly pendant. "It represents change for the better," he tells me as he helps me to put it on, and I blink away a few tears. We have a glass of champagne and then head to get dressed.

We work as a team to prepare Christmas dinner for six people. My auntie Joy and uncle Vernon are not coming over this year as they're spending it with Joy's family, and Mum tells me Margaret has got a new man with whom she'll be spending the day (he's a retired G.P. whose wife left him for a Greek waiter twenty years her junior; apparently Margaret has had a complete makeover and I wouldn't recognise her. *Good for her*, I think as I hear the story. *There's hope for us all*). Dad's friend Arthur is taking his new girlfriend up to Scotland to meet his family for the first time, and I'm pleased to hear that he's radiantly happy. Instead of last year's guests, we're expecting Tom's mum and dad.

They arrive at one. Nervously, I open the door to them, but I needn't have worried — they greet me warmly with hugs and, as I've put weight on lately, I have no fear of being told I'm all skin and bones like I was last year, not that Tom's parents would say anything so tactless.

Tom's mum hands us our presents and Mum leads them inside so we can hand over theirs. I offer them some drinks and we settle into relaxed conversation in the candle-filled living room, at which Tom's parents don't even bat an eyelid, having been around to the house before and being used to my mum's rapidly-changing hobbies.

Chapter Twenty-Six

Soon it's time to sit down for our Christmas dinner, and I help to place the steaming dishes on the table that I set earlier. Everyone *oohs* their appreciation as the turkey is put down in the centre, and Dad starts carving. I get déjà vu as Wizard plays on the stereo.

The conversation flows as we eat. Anne and Tom Senior tell us stories about Tom from his childhood, and I laugh as I picture a smaller version of him falling out of trees and eating sand. Mum and Dad join in with some anecdotes from my own youth, and I cringe humorously at reminders of the time I decided to put makeup on the cat and the time I fell off the stage in a school assembly while I was in the middle of a solo.

We move on to dessert, and this year everyone manages to finish their Christmas pudding and custard.

I thought it might be awkward as Tom's parents have been used to having Melanie in their lives for so long, but as she helps us to clear away the dishes, Anne hugs me and tells me that she's never seen Tom look at anyone the way that he looks at me, and I blush and glance over at him, where he's watching with a smile.

We settle back into the living room with our drinks (don't worry, reader, I've paced myself this year) and we play a few board games with a break to watch the King's speech. Then Mum persuades me to finally have a Tarot card reading. I used to be terrified of hearing something bad was going to happen, however much I was sceptical about fortune-telling, but I was even more terrified about hearing something *good*. It's the good things that make your heart sing and lull you into a false sense of security, and I had learned the hard way how your hopes and dreams can be dashed in an instant, and how soul-crushingly difficult it can be to pick yourself back up, and to put the pieces back together after a fall from a high place.

But this year I'm less fragile, and so I finally agree to the reading. We all sit around the dining table again, and Mum begins by dealing a series of cards from the deck and placing them in an arrangement of three that she calls a 'spread'. She tells me that the first card represents the past, the second the present, and the third, the future. She calls this 'The Three Fates.' I look at the cards she's dealt. The first depicts a dark figure bent in what appears to be sadness; she labels this one 'The Five of Cups'. The second is clearly a woman, who reminds me of Botticelli's Venus, and she calls this 'The Empress'. And the third is a pair of open hands with a wand between them, which she names 'The Ace of Wands'.

I look at her in bemusement, but she's too busy frowning down at the cards, her lips pursed. Everyone is craning forwards in their seats to watch, and I start to feel curious about what she'll say the cards might mean.

"Well?" I ask after a while.

She hesitates. "Remember, I'm only an amateur, and the

cards are open to interpretation. I'm not even sure that I deal them properly, to be honest ..."

I look at her in surprise as she says this. It's not like Mum to doubt herself. I glance at Tom, and he frowns and shakes his head. My heart sinks at the expectation of bad news, but then I remind myself that I don't even believe in this nonsense and give myself a shake.

"Just tell me, Mum," I say matter-of-factly, and brace myself for a tale of woe.

"Well ... I would say that the first card definitely indicates grief in your past – a loss, and great sadness ... perhaps a sense of betrayal of some kind," she frowns as she says this last point, but I inhale sharply. I've never told my parents about Matt's affair.

"What about the second?" Tom asks curiously.

"I don't – I'm not sure ..." she looks at me sharply and bites her lip.

"It's okay, Mum, just spit it out," I tell her impatiently, and she takes a breath.

"Well ... The Empress is the divine feminine, the source from which life springs. It can represent fertility, even ... pregnancy and motherhood," she finishes in a rush, and I blink.

"What about the third?" Anne asks eagerly.

"The Ace of Wands ... that could be a passionate relationship, a new beginning ... male energy ... in context with The Empress, perhaps a male ... birth." And she looks at me with a mix of anxiety and hope on her face.

I sit, stunned, for a minute, and then burst into tears. Everyone jumps out of their seats and rushes around to me to comfort me. Tom gets to me first and he crouches down beside me, talking to me in a gentle voice. My mum is beside herself, wringing her hands and apologising. Dad is rubbing my back and Tom's parents are making soothing comments nearby.

Someone hands me a tissue, and I blow my nose noisily, but more tears flow. I can't stop them.

"Oh, I never should have put pressure on you to have a reading," Mum wails, and I shake my head.

"It's not that, Mum," I tell her through my tears, and then I blurt out, "It's that I've just realised that my period's late."

There's a collective intake of breath, and then Tom asks in a sharp voice, "How late?"

"*Very* late," I tell him. I look at his face; his eyes are glittering intensely but I can't work out the expression in them. All of a sudden, he jumps up and rushes out the house. Everyone exclaims. His dad follows after him quickly, but before he can even get out the front door, we hear an engine start and the car peeling off the driveway. Within seconds, the sound diminishes to nothing as he drives away.

"Oh, my God!" I say into the silence, and everyone rushes to comfort me, shell-shocked.

"I'll grab my car keys and follow him," his dad finally says, but – emotionlessly – I tell him to leave him.

Nobody seems to know what to do after that, so Mum and Anne bustle about making cups of tea for everyone and then we sit around drinking in near silence. Dad and Tom Senior try to make small-talk, but it soon fizzles out. The latter decides to try calling Tom on his phone, but it goes straight to voicemail. Tea-time arrives, and Mum cobbles together a little buffet which hardly anyone touches.

Anne and Tom Senior are just getting ready to make a subdued exit when we hear an engine approaching. Mum hurries over to the window and peeks around the curtain.

"It's him!" she exclaims, and I take a deep breath.

She opens the door to him, and he rushes past her and looks around for me. He spots me and walks over to me, then crouches down and holds out a brown paper bag. Confused, I take it from him slowly and look inside. It's a pregnancy test. I look up at him uncertainly and his eyes are glowing with hope. I burst into tears again and slap him on the arm.

"You scared the shit out of me running away like that!" I shriek, and an appalled look comes over his face.

"Oh, God! I didn't think …" he reaches for me.

"No, you bloody *didn't* think!" I tell him, snuffling snot back unattractively. Anne fetches me a fresh tissue and I blow my nose noisily. Dad starts chuckling, and Tom Senior joins in. Soon, my mum and Anne are giggling too, and I don't know if it's in relief or just a release of emotion, but I finally see the funny side too. Tom looks at us like we've all gone mad, and that makes me laugh even harder. I wipe at the fresh tears of laughter coming out of my eyes, and I reach for him and hug him tightly.

As the laughter subsides, he murmurs in my ear, "Are you going to keep me in suspense?"

I take a deep breath and bite my lip, and he takes my hand and leads me out of the room. Our parents watch us go with anxious but hopeful expressions, and I see my mum take Anne's hand. We go to the bathroom upstairs, and he waits while I read the instructions and then pee on the stick.

He holds me while we wait the few minutes until the little window changes, then we both hold our breaths and clasp hands as we look down on it. The word PREGNANT stands out boldly, and I clap my free hand over my mouth. He grabs me in a bear hug and starts crying unashamedly, and that sets me off again. We stay like that for some time, and he murmurs to me about how happy I've made him, and how much he loves me, and how we're going to be a family.

"I love you too," I tell him tearfully, and he kisses me passionately.

Eventually, we head downstairs, hand-in-hand. Our parents are waiting anxiously on the sofas, but as soon as we enter the room smiling, they greet us with a mix of gasps and cheers. Anne and Mum rush forward to hug us and our fathers follow behind them. Dad has tears in his eyes, and Mum and Anne are outright blubbering. Tom Senior congratulates us huskily, and I can tell he's choking back a few tears of his own.

"It's still early days," I remind them, but Mum's already talking about taking up knitting so she can make some baby clothes, and Anne's asking me if I've had any morning sickness. Tom has a new energy in his step, and he's already started to coddle me. I laugh at him as he plumps a cushion for me and encourages me to sit down.

Dad pours champagne for everyone (orange juice for me) and we toast to a wonderful Christmas present. Anne and Tom Senior stay for the rest of the evening before they reluctantly decide it's time to head home.

It's after nine, and I'm bushed. Mum waves me away when I try to help tidy up and Tom scoops me into his arms and carries me like a bride up the stairs while Mum and Dad chuckle and call, "Good night!" after us.

"Carrying me again?" I say to him with a twinkle in my eye as he climbs.

"You keep giving me excuses. This is the best one yet, though." We reach the top of the stairs and he stops to kiss me.

"It's not too soon?"

"Not for me."

"Me neither," I smile, and he smiles happily and continues on to the bedroom.

The next day, we set out on our traditional Boxing Day walk. We take Sammy, Mum and Dad's collie, and Tom throws his ball for him as we amble. He chases after it with boundless enthusiasm, retrieving it and returning it to him, panting eagerly, and we laugh as Tom picks up the drool-covered toy and tosses it for the umpteenth time. The crisp air is invigorating, and I feel a sense of peace as we progress through the fields in our wellies. I can tell that Mum and Dad are happy to see me content, and I link arms with them as we watch Sammy go sniffing along a hedgerow.

Later that morning, we pack up our things and kiss them

goodbye, then head over to Tom's parents' house. I'm going to meet his sister and her family for the first time, but I feel excited rather than nervous.

The door opens before we get there and a toddler comes squealing and waddles over the threshold trying to escape. Tom laughs and scoops him up, and greets his sister who comes up behind with a kiss. Her name's Beth, and she smiles warmly at me as she turns to me. We hug, and she leads us inside where I meet her husband, Ray, and their daughter, Poppy.

Anne offers us some drinks, and I notice that Beth also asks for an orange juice. Tom and I play with the children while we chat with the adults, and then Anne declares that lunch is ready. While we eat, Beth announces that she's pregnant again, twelve weeks, and we congratulate her, but she catches the knowing looks that pass between Tom's parents and me and Tom, and frowns.

"What?" she asks curiously.

Tom looks at me with raised eyebrows and I nod and wink and he announces our news. She claps her hands and rushes out of her seat to hug us.

"We'll be pregnancy buddies!" she exclaims happily. "I haven't had one before."

I smile but caution her that it's still early days for me, but I can tell that she's excited. She starts informing me about the best places to buy baby clothes and pushchairs, and her enthusiasm is infectious.

"We've decided to hire a nanny part-time with this one," she confides in me as I help to clear away the dishes after the meal's over. "I don't know if you know that I've struggled with post-natal depression."

I tell her about Jemima, and my own struggles with my mental health, and she clasps my hand. "Even more reason to support each other through this," she tells me earnestly, and I hug her.

Tom and I stay for a little longer before we say our goodbyes and head back to London. We'll be returning for the New Year – Brenda has invited us all to another of her parties – and on the drive home, Tom tells me that he hopes she gets everyone playing the Suck and Blow game again. I roll my eyes but grin at him.

He asks me when the tenancy is up on my flat and when I query why he wants to know, he asks me to move in with him.

"I'm practically living at yours anyway," I tell him.

"I know but I want to make it official."

"Okay then," I answer, pleased, and he takes my hand and kisses it.

We spend the week transferring my belongings to his place. The tenancy is up in January anyway so now's as good a time as any to make the move. However, I find the time to meet up with Lucy before we head back for Brenda's party.

We go to the Italian by my flat and she shows me the twelve-week scan. We gush over the details that are already clear – the head and nose, a leg, and an arm raised as if waving. I sigh, and Lucy looks at me in sympathy.

"You'll be having one of these before you know it," she

tells me softly, and I bite my lip.

"Maybe sooner than you think."

She blinks and stares at me, hard. "Are you saying what I think you're saying?"

I nod, and she squeals.

"Oh my God! I'm so happy for you! Does Tom know? Of course he does or you wouldn't be telling me – would you?" she blabbers, and I laugh and tell her that he knows. "How did he take it?"

I recount the story of the Tarot cards and how Tom rushed out of the house, and she listens agog at all the details.

"Bloody hell!" she says when I finish. "Well, that's one for the grandkids."

"I know, right?"

I tell her about Beth and tentatively suggest that the three of us could get together sometimes before and after the babies are born – maybe even invite Jemima, too.

"Good idea – we can keep each other sane," Lucy responds.

"My thoughts exactly."

We finish our meals, while Lucy rabbits on enthusiastically about going to antenatal classes together and attending baby groups, and I have to remind her more than once that it's still early days for me.

"I know, I know – I'm just so damn excited." And I can't help feeling more than a little excited myself, reader.

Chapter Twenty-Seven

The taxi bumps up the long drive and the smell of manure assaults my nose as I climb out. All of the lights in Brenda's house are blazing and seventies music is pumping out through the open door. Currently, The Jackson 5 are ordering *Don't Stop 'til You Get Enough* and I smile at Tom.

Brenda screams and coming running, her blonde perm bouncing, when she sees my mum walk through the door and into the open-plan living area, and Mum screams back. They hug and air kiss, and Bob comes over and shakes my dad's hand. They look at their wives in exasperation, but I know how important female friendship is and I think it's sweet. Brenda turns to me next and, with a 'Hello, sweetheart!', she embraces me in a warm hug. As usual, she smells like vanilla and childhood.

Brenda gives me a knowing look as she greets Tom just as enthusiastically and then she's gossiping with Mum while barely pausing for breath. Tom and I leave Dad with Bob and go and greet his parents before heading to the drinks table.

"Which do you think's best?" I ask him, "*Planes, Trains and Automobiles* or *Home Alone?*"

He looks at me askance as he grabs an apple juice for me and a beer for himself. "*Planes, Trains and Automobiles*, and if your answer is different, I might have to re-think this relationship."

I laugh and reassure him.

We mingle with the guests, including my old headmistress and the vicar, who are apparently still having an affair and which of course the whole of the county knows about, but they themselves still think is a big secret.

While we're talking to one of Brenda's neighbours, *Let's Get it On* starts playing and it takes me back to a year ago when Tom entered the party and nearly caught me stuffing a million mini sausages into my mouth. I look over at him and bite my lip, and his eyes heat as he stares back.

Fortunately (or not), Brenda announces that the buffet's open then. While we queue up for the food, I'm reminded of Melanie, and I ask if he's heard how she's doing.

"She's doing well apparently – she's started seeing a new teacher at her school. Mum's still in touch with her parents so she hears all the gossip."

We get to the front of the queue and we both reach for a vol-au-vent at the same time. He smirks and I stuff one into his mouth making him nearly choke.

Both sets of parents are already sitting down, eating with Brenda and Bob, so once we've piled up our plates we join them.

"Will there be any party games tonight?" Tom enquires innocently as we sit munching on quiche and pork pies, and I roll my eyes at him.

"Oh, yes!" Brenda replies enthusiastically. "I thought I'd try some different ones out this year though."

"That's a shame," he murmurs so only I can hear.

We finish our food, and Brenda announces the first game. To my surprise, she declares that we're going to play musical chairs. Tom's eyes light up like a child's and he rushes to help some of the others gather enough chairs. Because there are a lot more people than chairs available, Brenda decides that we'll do a few different rounds.

Tom and I are in the second round, and after the music stops for the fourth time, I find myself without a chair. Tom quickly pulls me down onto his lap and we laugh as people accuse him good-naturedly of cheating. Of course, he goes on to win.

The next game is another children's party favourite – pass the parcel. But Brenda assures us all that there are gifts for adults inside each layer. I sit in a circle next to Tom, feeling a little bit silly (remember, I haven't had a drink, reader!), but no one else seems to bat an eyelid.

The music starts, and we pass the parcel around. It arrives in my hands, and the music stops. Feeling a little excited (perhaps I am a big kid after all), I rip off the wrapper and discover a miniature bottle of Wild Spirit's flavoured vodka – the one that our agency produced the ad for earlier in the year. I won't be able to drink it for a while yet, but I smile at the reminder of the first campaign I worked on. The music starts again, and I pass the remainder of the parcel on.

It does another round and then the music again stops on

me. I try to hand it on to the next person but they insist it landed on me, so I guiltily start tearing another layer off. This time, I discover a bag of nachos inside. I look at Tom in amusement, and he smiles back, and then the music starts up again.

When it lands on me again and the music stops for the third time in a row, I'm at first confused and then I start to get a little suspicious. I look around at everyone but they all look back innocently. I look at Tom quizzically but he just urges me to hurry up before the music starts again. I tear open the wrapper and discover a fridge magnet depicting Van Gogh's *Starry Night Over the Rhone*, and now I look at Tom accusingly. He chuckles, and the music starts playing so I pass the parcel on. I look around, and everyone's smiling at me now. I shake my head, but I can't help grinning as I wait for the present to do the circuit.

Surprise, surprise, Tom passes the parcel on to me and the music stops. I laugh, and everyone cheers, and I rip open the wrapper. This time it's a bracelet, with numbered charms strung along it that make '27+53'. I roll my eyes at Tom happily and again pass the parcel on as the music re-starts.

The next layer reveals a copy of the book *Little Red Riding Hood* which gains more than a few puzzled glances, but Tom and I share a secret smile before the music again forces me to pass the parcel along.

The parcel has shrunk a lot by this time, and there can only be a couple of layers left. I watch in anticipation as it gets passed around, smiling at my mum and dad and Tom's parents when it gets to them, and they grin back excitedly. It arrives in my hands, and once again the music stops and we all laugh. I tear it open to reveal a CD of *Nights in White Satin* and my eyes prick with tears as I remember dancing at Lucy's wedding. I lean over and kiss Tom and everyone cheers.

The music starts for what I sense is the last time, and I begin to tremble. The parcel seems to take ages to get back to me, but when it does, of course, the music stops. There's a hush in the room as I rip open the wrapper and I inhale sharply as I discover a small jewellery box. Tom takes it out of my hand and pulls me up into a standing position and then he kneels before me holding the box open to reveal a diamond ring.

I put my trembling hand over my mouth as he starts speaking.

"Pippa Clayton, you're everything I want and need for the rest of my life. I would wait for you forever, but you would make me the happiest man alive if you would agree to wear this ring from this day on, and start the New Year as my fiancée. Beautiful Pippa, will you marry me?" His voice cracks at the end, and I nod and croak 'Yes' as tears spill down my cheeks. There's a collective 'Aah!' from the other guests, and they break into a round of applause as he puts the ring on my finger and stands to kiss me lingeringly, and then everyone's gathering around us to congratulate us. I reach out to my mum and dad, and they hug me tight and say, "Congratulations, darling!" and then Tom's parents are there and we do the same.

The music re-starts, and it's *Do the Conga* by Black Lace. I laugh at the cheesy number as Tom and I are dragged into a line and all of the guests start dancing through the house and then out in a circle around the farmhouse and back into the house again.

Tom pulls me down onto the sofa when the song finishes but most people stay up dancing to the next song, which is *Agadoo*. He puts his arm around me and kisses me.

"You've been very naughty," I break away to tell him.

"I could have been naughtier," he murmurs into my ear. "I considered putting a spanking paddle in."

"You didn't!"

He laughs, and I'm pretty sure he's joking, but not one hundred percent.

We sit on the sofa chatting and kissing, and accepting congratulations from the people who couldn't get to us earlier, and then midnight's looming and we all gather in the requisite circle for the countdown. Tom kisses my breath away when we get to zero and he's still kissing me when everyone else bursts into *Auld Lang Syne*. I hear fireworks going off but I can't tell if they're in the distance or in my head, and then we break away and everyone's wishing us a Happy New Year.

"They're right, you know," Tom murmurs to me.

"About what?"

"It *is* going to be a happy New Year." And he kisses me once again.

Epilogue

An invisible band begins tightening around my swollen middle, and I take a breath to prepare myself.

"Another one," I gasp, clutching Tom's hand and simultaneously reaching for the gas and air. My hair is stuck to my head with sweat and I'm not sure I have the energy for much more of this, but I dig down deep and pray for the strength to endure for just a little bit longer.

Tom brushes the hair back off my forehead as I breathe through the pain. "You're doing so, so well," he tells me soothingly. He has dark shadows beneath his eyes and he seems to feel every contraction with me judging by the way he grimaces in sympathy every time.

The contraction passes and I pull the mask away. The midwife decides to check how far along I am.

"Good news," she says from between my legs. "You're at ten centimetres."

I breathe a sigh of relief. "Does that mean it's nearly over?" I ask desperately. Beth had a very quick labour with her little girl, but Lucy had said it was *bad* when she gave birth to her baby boy. However, hearing about it and experiencing it are two totally different things.

"The second stage can last anywhere between twenty minutes and a couple of hours," she answers matter-of-factly.

"I'm not sure I can manage another couple of hours," I tell her anxiously.

"We'll help you get through it."

I feel my abdomen begin to squeeze again. "Here it comes!" I tell them.

They help me into a kneeling position and I start breathing into my mask yet again. The midwife coaches me through the contraction calmly until the pain thankfully begins to recede.

We do this several times until, at last, the urge to push is so overwhelming that the midwife tells me to go for it. I make a guttural, animal noise that I barely recognise as myself while a burning sensation stings me between my legs. I pant as I feel the baby slide out and hear Tom saying, "Oh, God, oh Jesus" over and over again.

I turn to get my first look at our baby boy, and see his red, wrinkled face contorted as he screams healthily. I laugh and reach for him and the midwife places him against my chest. I look at Tom, who's staring at us in awe, then I look back down at the baby because I can't bear to take my eyes off him for too long.

"You did it, sweetheart. You were amazing," Tom breathes as he kisses first me and then our little boy.

"*We* did it," I tell him.

Printed in Great Britain
by Amazon

14550396R00149